To C...
wo

CH00642507

June 2023

WHAT THE WIND SAW

1:25

35

SHORT STORIES FROM THE HEART OF HERTFORDSHIRE

ZOË JASKO

Printed edition:
Also available in multiple e-book formats.

Published by:
The Endless Bookcase Ltd,
Suite 14 STANTA Business Centre, 3 Soothouse Spring,
St Albans, Hertfordshire, AL3 6PF, UK.

More information can be found at:
www.theendlessbookcase.com.

ISBN: 978-1-914151-41-5

Author photo by **Andrew Mason**

Map of 'Middle Hertfordshire', cover design and section image design by **Stephen Hill**

For

Peter Waine

Who helped with this book in so many ways

ABOUT THE AUTHOR

Zoë has lived in beautiful places including Devon and the French Alps, but it is the picturesque and comfortable lanes, fields and villages of the Hertfordshire countryside around where she has brought up her family, that has provided the inspiration for *What the Winds Saw*. A trained singer, she is co-founder and creative director of the Hertfordshire based Felici Opera.

Zoë has a BA in French and History (University of Exeter) and an MA in Victorian Studies – 19ᵗʰ Century art, history, and literature (Birkbeck College, University of London). She has been an active member of a marvellous book club since 2008.

www.zoejasko.com

Photo credit:
Andrew Mason

ENDORSEMENTS AND REVIEWS

"Zoë Jasko creates a wonderfully evocative atmosphere through these stories inspired by the history, folklore and landscape of the remarkable county of Hertfordshire. Turning points are explored through the personal, everyday lives of its residents past, present and future that we can all relate to."

Emma Harper
Curator, Welwyn-Hatfield Museum Service

"Beautifully written and very lyrical like the musician that you are. The writing made me feel safe and warm".

Lucy Gravatt
Journalist and Communications Director

"These stories are extraordinary, each one a mini masterpiece, each competing to be a personal favourite. Each is somehow spiritual in its own way. The reader enters a field, turns a corner and watches a mini play, with different sets and from different periods. Beware the casual reader; the stories are deceptively simple. It is easy to access the stories at different levels and each is fulfilling. What I am trying to say at midnight is that I have never read a book quite like this one. The small area of England comes to life, is populated by those in the stories and no one can visit, seek out, those spots and not think of these stories and wonder if perhaps they were all true at some moment in time, two thousand years ago, 50 years ago, or at a moment which corresponds with no time as we measure it in conventional terms."

Peter Waine
Author and former national chairman of CPRE

FOREWORD

How wonderful to have so many fascinating short stories written about one's own county in one great book. That is exactly what we have in *What the Wind Saw*.

Hertfordshire is The County of Opportunity, but it is also one of great diversity – possibly the most diverse county in the country. What we learn from Zoë Jasko's book is that this has always been the case throughout history.

Having a glimpse of the history that surrounds Middle Hertfordshire through numerous stories spanning many centuries is entertaining but at the same time educational. The way in which Zoë Jasko brings history to life in each story is wonderful and to know that these are stories taking place on my own doorstep makes it more poignant. And there is even a story about my boyhood hero – the great archaeologist Sir Mortimer Wheeler.

Separating into the four parts – Villages, Towns, The City and Fields, Land and River adds to the interest and like many with each story I have been saying to myself… "I know these places well."

In future, I will wonder what the wind blowing through the trees of Hertfordshire has seen…

Robert Voss CBE CStJ
HM Lord-Lieutenant of Hertfordshire

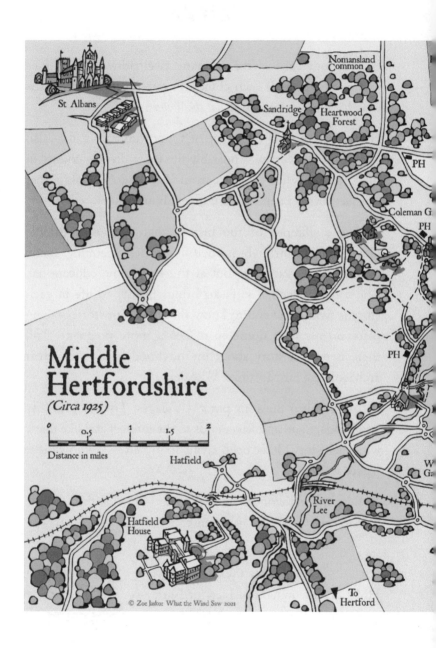

Middle
Hertfordshire

(Circa 1925)

0   0.5   1   1.5   2

Distance in miles

St Albans

Nomansland
Common

Sandridge

Heartwood
Forest

PH

Coleman G

PH

PH

Hatfield

W
Ga

River
Lee

Hatfield
House

© Zoe Jasko: What the Wind Saw 2021

To
Hertford

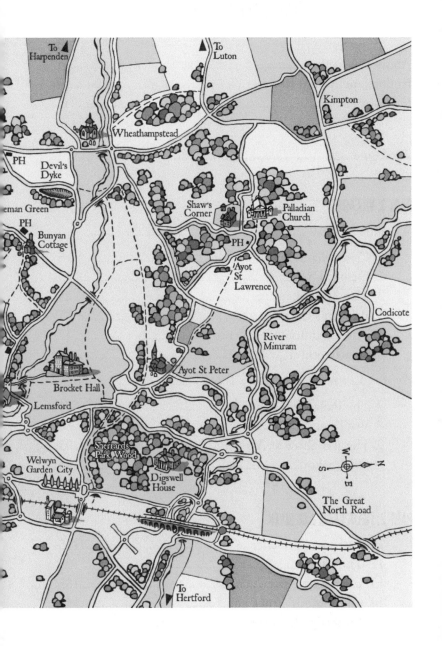

WHAT THE WIND SAW

About the Author i
Endorsements and Reviews ii
Foreword iii

Prologue 1

PART 1: VILLAGES

Wheathampstead 3

    1. Cassivellaunus 5
    2. Devil's Dyke 15
    3. The Airfield 25
    4. Bunyan's Cottage 37
    5. The Common of Adventure 47
    6. Heartwood 59

Ayot St Lawrence 69

    7. The Palladian Church 71
    8. Vodka and Lead 83
    9. The Art Show at Ayot 95
    10. Pygmalion 103

PART 2: FIELD, LANE, AND RIVER

    11. Paths of Pestilence 115
    12. The River 125
    13. Oxblood 135
    14. Catch Me If You Can! 143
    15. Butterfly Memories 153

PART 3: TOWNS

Hatfield 163

    16. Guns for Mosquitos 165
    17. The Girl under the Oak 175

Welwyn Garden City 185

    18. The Man Who Took His Pig for a Walk 187
    19. The Woman Who Lost Her Voice (The Muses) 199
    20. Digswell House 209
    21. The Birthday 221
    22. Olivia's Apple Tree 231

PART 4: THE CITY

St Albans 243

    23. Proserpina's Promise 245
    24. Bleak House 253
    25. Gladys 263

Epilogue **275**
Acknowledgements **279**

PROLOGUE

I know this county like the back of my hand. This river, just here, look! the Lea – see how it winds its way through the fields and woodland to Wheathampstead where Julius Caesar fought the great Cassivellaunus. Now look here to the Abbey on the hill, that's where your country created its first Christian martyr – Alban. Hold my hand, just for a few seconds, and here, now, do you see it? the Hatfield oak where a young, imprisoned heir learned she would be Queen? Keep your eyes wide open or you'll miss it. Don't blink. Quick! look down there, do you see the students spilling from the campus buildings? A University now but just a few seconds ago the land beneath was the launchpad for four thousand mosquitos to take to the skies.

Ssh ssh! What do you hear? The waves in the trees? The trees in the waves? Or is it nothing – stillness – silence?

I have seen it all. I have heard it all – before. All. Before.

Heorotfrodsir – rolls off the tongue, doesn't it? Hertfordshire.

I saw it arrive. I brought it on a black cloud. I carried the merchants and the sailors who bore the fleas on their clothes, on the backs of the rats on the ships. I filled the sails and carried the pestilence to England. I touched the bodies of the ill and the immune and saw the boils and pustules. I carried the cries of the dying and the tears of the grieving, the bells tolling. I carried the silence.

When the sickness had finished eating the population so much had changed. Although few could count, it seemed that half the world was buried leaving the remaining half to demand more payment for their labour and to claim their liberty. How strange that death was the price for freedom to seek life elsewhere. Time covered the dead villages into mounds and I helped, laying soil and leaves whilst I watched the villages that lived.

"Complicit!" I hear you cry. No, don't forget, it is as I told you, I have seen it before. Take the Romans. I helped them on their journey too. How else did they reach Britannia from Gaul? Surely you don't think they rowed? Great villas with beautiful mosaics and hypocausts they built, roads and bridges. But they left. The Roman Empire withdrew and I helped Time cover its tracks. I spread the grass seed. I blew the Hawthorne. I felled the weaker trees and allowed the saplings to find new homes. I took the bee to the flower, showed the bird its nest. I will be here fiercer with breath of fire or of ice – you choose – when you have brought your world to the brink of destruction by burning your fuels.

I see you as you walk in this land as I visit the villages, the fields, the towns, the city. I am the air that you breathe, the gas you exhale. I know your thoughts and your fears, your loves, and your triumphs. I see the hidden things which you cannot see but which have always shaped this land. I touch your cheek when you cry and spin the falling autumn leaf for you to catch and make your wish.

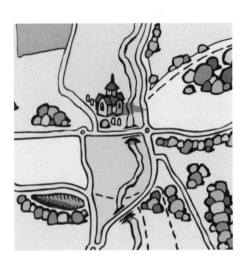

PART 1: VILLAGES
WHEATHAMPSTEAD

1.

CASSIVELLAUNUS

A breeze toyed with the calf's hide opening to the tent and through it, the man imprisoned within could make out the leg hair and scabbards of the two soldiers who stood guard over him. The sound of horses whinnying and the harsh scrape of stone sharpening a metal blade were the only signs of the soldiers and prisoners invisible to him beyond the tent's mouth.

The day was bright outside, but inside it was dark. He had been held in here for many hours now and his eyes had become used to the gloom. A candle on the table flickered in the draught, creating shadows that fought with those made by the daylight filtering in at the calf's hide opening. Furs carpeted the floor. A standard, not his own, took the position of a throne, dominating the interior; a golden eagle effigy, the might of Rome.

A piece of bread and a lump of goat's cheese remained untouched on the plate which a guard had delivered not yet an hour ago. An empty cup and a full pitcher of mead stood alongside it. Cassivellaunus rose stealthily from where he had been sitting quietly on the bench, observing the hidden blades of the guards at the entrance. Without a sound, he moved to the table and snatched the bread from the plate. He stuffed it angrily into his mouth, as if he had been waiting in ambush and was now making a swift and deadly attack. He wiped the crumbs from his lips with his leather wristband.

Silently, he moved to the entrance, where he stood motionless, looking down at his strong hands. He clenched his right hand tight and looked down at his knuckled fist. It was a rock. He could use it to pound the nearest guard. By taking the pair by surprise, he could wrest their blades from their scabbards before they even had the chance to draw. He could plunge the steel into their soft flesh and make his escape. He was so close to their bodies on the other side of the flapping calf's hide, that he could smell their stale odour, he could breathe their breath. The regular tap-scrape-tap of stone against blade persisted in the background, a macabre bird song in the landscape.

But ambush now would be suicide and suicide was not his battle plan. He had too much cunning. Cassivellaunus, leader of the strong and terrible Catuvellauni, uncurled his fist slowly, finger by finger.

He returned to the table and picked up the goat's cheese and ate, this time slowly, ponderously. The golden eagle standard was his dining companion, golden feathers gleaming in the candlelight.

"What kind of man are you, Caesar?" he asked the eagle under his breath.

The eagle did not reply. It stared pointedly forward with its lifeless golden eyes.

Cassivellaunus knew the answer. Julius Caesar was a man such as himself – a man of power and passion, of lusts and deceits. If Caesar was an eagle, then he, Cassivellaunus, was a falcon. They were both akin, two birds of prey, ruling their skies, ruthlessly. Today, at this hour, at this point in the history of his land, the eagle may have the falcon caught by its tailfeathers, pinning its rival to the ground by its mighty claws, but the falcon had trounced the eagle before. It could do so again.

Not so long ago, when the Roman army had crossed from Gaul, landing their boats on the shores of the southern coast and the legions had marched north in arrogance, the Britons had waited. They had refused to be drawn into battle. Instead, they drew the invading force inland, and flirted with them, daring them to cross the estuary of the river Tems, portraying themselves as a weak maiden easily plucked on the other side of the water. When the invaders rushed forward in their lust, their ships were pierced by the Britons' stakes planted just below the waterline. Caesar departed – defeated.

But an eagle will not stay away, not where it senses prey for the taking. Caesar returned with greater forces, more legions, more ships, more cavalry. He pushed northwards, advancing unchecked on the lands of the Catuvellauni. Britons are fickle friends. The neighbouring tribes, the Cenimagni, the Segontiaci, the Ancalites, the Bibroci, the Cassi, all threw in their lot with the enemy and led Caesar to Wheathampstead and so to Cassivellaunus. Backstabbing, murderous thieves – these once allies assisted the Romans in the slaughter of the Catuvellauni. In the woodland alongside the River Lea British blood had been spilt. In the great ditches, which the tribe had constructed generations before to protect themselves from such attack, life blood had flowed from body to mud, to water.

The tent flap parted and one of the two guards entered.

"Stand up," he barked in his foreign tongue, motioning to Cassivellaunus to rise from the bench. Cassivellaunus did so, but in no great hurry, and with indifference rather than with respect. The guard sneered at his prisoner and gripped his blade tighter.

"Caesar comes," the guard announced.

The calf's hide tent flap parted for a second time and a tired man with a thin face entered. His skin was pulled tight across his features as if there was not enough flesh to accommodate the unusual square shape of his skull. His bird-like eyes pierced the gloom of the tent, searching for the prisoner.

A second man followed behind; a weasel-faced man with an arrogant look in his dark eyes. He waited at Caesar's shoulder, assessing Caesar's stance towards the prisoner and the prisoner's response to Caesar. Cassivellaunus recognised the weasel, it was Commius, the client King of the Atrebate tribe, they had met before and their mutual contempt was profound.

The eagle and the falcon locked gaze; seconds passed. Caesar motioned to the guard to bring him his seat, a carved wooden chair covered in furs, that had been positioned unobtrusively in the corner of the tent. The weasel-faced man placed a stool next to Caesar for himself to sit on. The furniture arranged, Caesar indicated without words for the two men to take their seats.

Caesar sat calmly, his eyes never leaving the face of the prisoner King. To Cassivellaunus, his captor did not seem a typical soldier, he was not brawny and muscular, he did not radiate energy and action. His scrawniness was surprising, he seemed more a fledgling chick than an Emperor of the sky.

"You may begin," Caesar said to Commius in an unknown knot of sounds and then sat back in his chair, to be entertained by the combat or to be judge and jury at the test now set.

"Cassivellaunus, Caesar wishes to treat with you," weasel-faced Commius began.

"Is that so, Commius? You do surprise me!" replied Cassivellaunus, his words laced with sarcasm.

"I will lay out the terms," Commius replied, ignoring the Briton chief's scorn.

"As you please."

"Caesar demands tribute and hostages."

"No doubt."

Cassivellaunus kept his eyes fixed on Caesar during the exchange until he was certain that his captor could not understand the language Commius spoke.

"How much tribute?" Cassivellaunus asked Commius.

"One in ten of the bags of coins in your treasury in the first instance."

That was worth indeed to be forced to part with, but not the worst of what Caesar was demanding.

"And hostages?" he asked on the edge of his breath.

"Your son and your nephews."

Cassivellaunus willed his body not to flinch at the Roman demand. Coinage would be irritating to lose, but gold could be plundered from elsewhere. His son and his nephew, no, nothing would make him give these up to Rome, nor would he show to Caesar what they meant to him.

"And you, Commius? What is in this arrangement for you?"

"Nothing more than the pleasure it gives me assist with your surrender."

Cassivellaunus had no belief in the snake's words.

"And none of the coinage? Not even a slice of power?" he said, his voice full of calm hatred.

"I will accept what it pleases Caesar to bestow on his humble servant," Commius replied smoothly.

"As you did before, when you humbly accepted to rule the Atrebate tribe, and benefit from their wealth. You are no more than a vile client."

"It will be as Caesar wishes."

Cassivellaunus saw it clearly now. Commius, Caesar's Gallic ally, a wheedling, power-hungry, pretend-servant, had greater ambitions than the lands of the Atrebates.

"The Catuvellauni?" he breathed incredulously, hardly daring to believe the gall of the man, to gain so much favour with Caesar, that Caesar would reward him with Cassivellaunus' own lands and people.

"Oh no, Cassivellaunus, Caesar is inclined to let you keep your tribe, if you pay him what he asks," Commius replied in his most pleasant and agreeable manner.

Perhaps, he was wrong then, perhaps the Atrebates' lands, pastures and coins satisfied Commius. Whatever murky scheme lay in Commius' mind, it was still hidden by mist.

"You may tell Caesar that I will grant him the coins, but I will not hand him my son and nephews. He asks too much."

Throughout the exchange Caesar had regarded both men quietly; still, as a fisherman waits for the trout to swim into the nets, as a hunter waits for the wild boar to approach within range of the throw of a spear. He was an observer. He was watching a play which he was directing.

The message translated, Caesar laid his hands flat on the table in front of him and stood up slowly.

"Tell Cassivellaunus I will let him keep his son but he must select fifty young men and fifty young women to take his son's place as hostages."

Commius translated Caesar's words to the sullen Briton, who took the pronouncement as one drinks sour wine or who has no choice but to eat rotting food.

"Come, Commius, we will leave him to consider for the time being. You will return to Cassivellaunus before noon to collect his answer and then bring it to me." Caesar ordered.

The two men exited the tent; Caesar carrying the cares of a great leader on his wizened brow, Commius with the smirk of a man used to rising through the fall of others.

When they had left, the vanquished king pulled his fingers into a tight fist, a rock with which to pound his enemy. He slammed it angrily against the palm of his other hand and ground the bone of his fingers against the flesh of his hand, imagining how he would grind Commius, how he would grind Caesar, if he could escape and call on Briton forces sill friendly towards him. Then, slowly, he uncurled each finger of his clenched fist one at a time, considering his options.

His pointing finger: to send secretly for aid from the Kings of Kent – Cingerotix, Carvilius, Taximagulus, and Segovax, they would have no wish to have Rome established here. A surprise attack could see the Romans chastened and forced to withdraw, but he would be indebted to these untrustworthy British allies.

His tall third finger: to accept the terms of surrender, make payment of coin and flesh, leaving his pride bruised but his kingdom intact.

His fourth ring finger: autumn was on the cusp of turning to winter, Caesar would surely be well advised to make a swift departure and to march his soldiers back to

Rome while the weather held. Cassivellaunus' tribute of gold and slave hostages would be sure to follow.

Or maybe not.

Cassivellaunus, King of the Catuvellauni kissed his fourth ring finger. His decision was made. He poured mead from the pitcher into the tankard and drank deeply. He would pretend to agree to the terms of the treaty, but he would never send the hostages, and would only send the gold if the Romans' presence on the British Isles was fully established – and that might never happen. With a smirk on his face that matched that of Commius', Cassivellaunus waited for that weasel-faced man to return for his answer.

2.
DEVIL'S DYKE

There is a village where time is not merely measured in the tens or hundreds of years but in the thousands. A village where our earliest brothers and sisters found shelter on the banks of the meandering Lea and where Roman and Saxon settlers forged communities. Our unknown forefathers worked the earth with their hands and shaped the contours of our landscape like a potter handling clay. Today, we work here at Wheathampstead as archaeologists uncovering their traces. For here was the stronghold of Cassivellaunus leader of the Catuvellauni, here he built the defences of his city and here he repulsed the attack of Julius Caesar recorded in the Commentari de Bello Gallico.

Mortimer Wheeler, Wheathampstead, September 1931

Her heart sank as she read his memo to the press and that horrible sick feeling she fought so often to keep in the pit of her stomach rose to her mouth. So he was going to do it. After all she had said, after all the arguments, he was going to do it. Yet the awful sickening conclusion, was that she knew that he had no choice. She carefully folded the paper and put it neatly inside the flap at the back of her notebook leaving both tidily on the site office desk and stepped out into the sunlight of the day.

She was an unusual figure on site; a tiny, dark-eyed, dark-haired intense woman of Irish descent with a ready smile of genuine warmth. Whatever the weather, she would always be dressed in a sensible brown suit and plain leather shoes – never the gamine trousers of the younger women. Although in age more of an older sibling to the university students, she exuded a maternal air and the younger generation turned to her both for her nurturing and her razor-sharp intellect.

"Good morning, Mrs Wheeler," a friendly voice greeted her, followed by several others. Tessa smiled, acknowledging each with a nod, and stopped to answer questions or offer advice.

"Excuse me, Mrs Wheeler, will Mr Wheeler be on site at all today?"

Tessa paused, nausea rising to her mouth, before turning and forcing herself to hold eye contact with the young blonde.

"No Josie, we are not expecting him today."

Tessa read disappointment in the girl's face and guilt in her eyes whilst her own countenance, with considerable effort, remained plastered with pleasantness and was inscrutable.

Despite the attraction of Josie, her husband had spent very little time in Roman Verulam, St Albans, that summer. This was Tessa's domain. Verulam was her kingdom. They both tacitly understood the success of their professional partnering. He, all action, charisma, a man of imagination and ambition, would create the project and lead its public face, bold in his determination to raise archaeology to the highest of academic disciplines. While she, little Tessa Verney Wheeler, would carefully lead the dig, collate, interrogate, teach and raise the next generation of archaeologists.

She surveyed the neat trenches stopping at building III, room 4 of insula II where her students had recently uncovered a small cavity made from terracotta tiles, where a Roman baby had been buried centuries ago.

"He'd be so interested in all this… if only he'd stay long enough to look properly," she thought sadly to herself.

She missed him. She missed his passion, their conversations deep into the night, their speculation, their planning, their conclusions, the excitement of making discoveries – together. St Albans was too close to London and to whichever current mistress he visited so regularly, who held him in her thrall more than the young Josie McDonald, Tessa his wife, and even his beloved archaeology. She tensed her lips to prevent the familiar gagging at the thought. On the odd days that he deigned to visit the site that summer he would often as not disappear for stretches at a time investigating the neighbouring landscape, seeking to understand what he called the historical context; he needed the wider picture while she held on to the detail.

"Tessa, Tessa you will never believe what I've found!" he burst out on his return to the site office one evening in late June. His handsome face glowed like the sunset, his cheeks ruddied by the warmth of the day and flattered by his ginger-fair hair. He was full of excited anticipation, wanting her to guess but desperate to spill the beans himself.

"I have no clue," Tessa replied laughing, her spirits raised, as always, by his energy.

"Proof, my dear Mrs Wheeler, proof that Cassivellaunus' stronghold was here, close to Verulam, as we suspected. I have found without doubt the place where Julius Caesar attacked and the Britons repulsed."

He spoke fast and energetically. Tessa found herself swept along in his river of enthusiasm. She felt seasick and reached out an imaginary arm to prevent herself from being pulled along in the swift current of his interpretation, grasping at the words she needed to steady herself.

"Proof?"

"Yes, my dear," he cried, seizing her by the waist and pulling her into an impromptu waltz around the site office crammed with crates of finds, so that her body whirled as much as her head.

"What proof?"

"Devil's Dyke."

"What on earth is that?"

"Exactly, my dear – earth – a huge pre-Roman dyke. I know this is where Cassivellaunus commanded. I can feel it in my bones."

In a bustle of energy he had borrowed a handful of her diggers and a few students, Josie among them, she thought ruefully, and had excavated the Wheathampstead site – without her.

She had challenged him.

"But you have no proof, no evidence, not one single artefact to prove that Caesar was there."

Mortimer Wheeler's eyes narrowed. This was the point when he did not appreciate his wife's attention to detail.

"Tessa," came the icy response, spelling it out to her as if she were a child. "We know that the Catuvellauni were in Hertfordshire. We know that Julius Caesar crossed the river Thames. The earthworks at Devil's Dyke are significant. It is only a case of putting two and two together. Caesar must have met Cassivellaunus here. No artefacts do not mean that the Romans were not here, it just means that we haven't yet found the artefacts. In any case, we need Hertfordshire to take more interest in what we are doing and this will make a good headline."

And there was the truth and the sting. A new and bold interpretation in the press by attractive, exciting Mortimer Wheeler would indeed create interest and as a result, public donations would come rolling in. These funds would continue to underpin the Verulum dig and lay the foundation for the museum. But his interpretation was neither accurate nor careful. She had built her whole archaeological career on accuracy and care. He was fabricating a lie, like the lies she had been forced to eat every day for years now. She had fought for her intellectual identity and achieved so much in her field, but it was only as his wife that she had the opportunity to do so. In a man's world, she had to be better than the best and so her professional integrity rested on truth in details, two basic necessities that Mortimer Wheeler so frequently moulded to his will.

"You more than anyone else know how everything we do needs funding," he barely refrained from shouting at her as he left for God knows where – his mistress, more countryside roaming. She hardly cared. The Devil take his dyke!

Mortimer Wheeler attacked the site path, letting the office door slam pointedly behind him. Irritated beyond expression, he marched hard through the excavations and headed up the hill to the town.

"Mr Wheeler, sir, can you…"

"Speak to Mrs Wheeler for God's sake," he snapped.

There was far too much to do and no time to waste in St Albans with Tessa; the warmth of Lucinda in her apartment behind Bond Street beckoned and after partaking of her delights, there was an assault to be made on his mountain of paperwork, not to mention the press engagements. It was just too bad that Tessa could be so disloyal.

Taking his seat on the train Mortimer Wheeler opened his pocket notebook to read again his notes on the Devil's Dyke. The motion of the train and his bad temper made the words swim. The train was so hot, so damned hot. He loosened his tie and then took it off altogether. Feeling no better he stood up and cajoled down the window, to let fresh air into the carriage. But the air was hot and solid. No welcome breeze for Mortimer Wheeler. He sunk to his seat and closed his eyes. Against his will, memories crowded into the space in his mind that slumber created for them.

He sees himself approaching the woodland at Wheathampstead, registering the land incline downwards beneath his feet. He feels the excitement of a small boy being taken by his nurse to a playfellow's birthday party. He pushes his way through the trees and shrubs that form a gateway barring the entrance to the mouth of the dyke. He is an archaeological explorer. Before him, he sees a high-sided ditch with saplings, scrub and nettles. He presses on, but the smell of the damp earth fills his nostrils so violently and vividly that he is forced to cover his nose and mouth with the crook of his arm to prevent the evil stench from entering his soul.

The Dyke is a not ditch. It is a trench. A trench with the reeking smell of death and misery. A great flash of light explodes in his brain.

"Help me, please God help me!" he hears himself whimper.

He remembers the cries of pain and agony. Unforgettable sounds of horror ring incessantly, unforgivingly, in his ears.

His senses are spinning as artillery shells, ammunition from the past, land with thunderous crashes in his imagination.

He steps blindly forward in this Dyke, this trench, his feet losing their grip, slipping on the mud. His heart races at a million beats per second forcing pounding blood to his ears. Beads of sweat break out on his forehead. He can't breathe. Desperately he pulls at his collar.

Get a grip. He must get a grip.

The smell of the wet earth and rotting undergrowth is overpowering. The odour conjures the memories of shattered bodies, lying as grotesque ninepins; the uniforms swallowed by mud and blood.

"Wheeler, constrain yourself, man," he barks at himself.

He inhales deeply, pulling the air into his lungs… seven… eight….nine… ten… trying to re-orientate his senses.

Where is he? The Passchendaele? No Devil's Dyke – an ancient trench, just a ditch, a Saxon earthwork.

What is he doing here? Looking for Cassivellaunus.

"Cassivellaunus and Caesar," ashen-faced he whispers to the Dyke.

The train rocked on its tracks on its way into London. Wheeler, fretting in his unrestful doze in the over-hot carriage, pulled unconsciously on his collar.

"Get a grip, must get a grip," he muttered.

He forced himself to open his eyes.

"…eleven…twelve…thirteen…"

And so, with deep breaths and archaeology Wheeler smothered memory and guilt. The guilt that haunted him every day. The guilt that he had lived when so many others, clever and better men than him, had perished. He owed it to them to make the most of every day that he had left allotted to him; to make the marks on the world that they would have made, if their lives had not been cut short murderously on the Fields of Flanders.

Cassivellaunus and Caesar, yes, they had been there at Wheathampstead. Undoubtedly. The Dyke had seen battle. So had he. He knew it. Undoubtedly.

He felt calm now. The motion of the train rocked him from side to side, soothingly, like a mother rocks her baby's cradle. The golden evening sunshine, magnified by the window-glass, was now pleasantly soporific. He allowed his eyelids to once again become heavy.

Tessa crept into his half slumber. Tessa with her pert, bright little face, her lively, intelligent eyes. Loyal, determined little Tessa. Their partnership was the bedrock of his success. He knew he needed her. His respect for her matched that he had for any man, more even. Her intellect was his equal and his anchor in an intense world in which he was driven to live every second as if it were his last; a world where the sexual gratification found in a new lover was the only physical pleasure that satisfied.

He roused himself to wakefulness and took his pencil from his jacket pocket. He wrote alongside his notes on Cassivellaunus and the Dyke, 'Tessa agrees.' It didn't matter whether she did – or did not.

London, April 1937

Dear Lord Brocket

    I am delighted to learn that you intend to make a gift of the landmark known as Devil's Dyke to the people of Hertfordshire in honour of His Majesty's coronation and it is with gratitude that I accept the invitation to attend the opening of the commemorative gates which you have had erected at the entrance to the Dyke. As for the inscription on the stone, my late wife Tessa Verney Wheeler would have agreed with me that it is correct to state: "This entrenchment is part of a British city built in the 1ˢᵗ Century B.C. It is probably here that Julius Caesar defeated the British King Cassivellaunus in 54BC."

    Yours sincerely
    Mortimer Wheeler

3.
THE AIRFIELD

Mum had left them both sandwiches for tea again. The white bread was already curling at the edges and a bluebottle fly was buzzing around the slivers of packet pink ham within. Next to the plates were two smallish green apples she had found in the fruit bowl – a last-minute addition to their meal and an attempt to remind them to eat healthily.

Jonny opened the fridge door and shut his eyes to absorb the welcome blast of cool air on his skin. Still with his eyes shut he groped his hand into the fridge, feeling his way past not very much, until his fingers touched the chill aluminium of the coke can. Treasure! He took the can out, closed the door, and opened his eyes. Now no one could accuse him of taking the last can, because he had not seen how many cans were not now left in the fridge.

He pressed the metal cold to his cheek, enjoying the sting on his flesh. Then he opened his can and drank it as fast as the gas would allow. He could hear his sister, Heather, playing in her bedroom overhead, better drink up fast before she came down and found out. Now her footsteps were thump-thumping on the stairs of their semi-detached house. He drained the last drops, squashed the can under the heel of his trainer, and pushed it into the depths of the kitchen bin.

"What are you doing?" Heather asked suspiciously as she entered the kitchen.

"Looking for food, like a wino, what do you think!" he countered.

"You don't need to look in the bin stupid, Mum's left us tea."

She walked to the counter and bit into one of the sandwiches and made a face. It was dry.

"I'm bored," she announced. "And hot."

Who wasn't hot? The hottest summer on record. It was insufferable. Heather didn't look like she could wear any less clothing without being indecent. Her yellow jersey shorts hardly descended lower than her knickers and her white spaghetti strap vest top showed most of her very small bra.

"Why don't we take our tea and go to the den, Jonny? It will be cool in the woods."

He thought for a moment. Dan had asked him to go and play in the Dyke this evening. The local kids had rigged up a tyre on a rope that swung from one of the trees growing high on the side of the great ditch called Devil's Dyke. It was fun to cling to the rope and swing across the trench and to try and jump off and land as close to the other side as possible. Scaredy-cats wouldn't manage and would cling on to the tyre, rocking forwards and backwards, and would only jump off when the rope slowed and they could jump down, sure of where they would land. It would be fun to go with Dan to the Dyke, and cool, as the trees growing on the sides offered a welcome canopy of shade. Except that Michael Gregory would be there. Jonny had fought Michael last week and Michael had come off the worst with a black-eye and swearing revenge. Ordinarily, Jonny would have relished a tussle, but this evening he couldn't be bothered. It was just too hot.

"Alright," he agreed.

Heather locked the door. Mum had fixed the key to a string of ribbon after Heather had lost the key for a second time from her shorts pockets when playing. She hung it around her neck like a piece of jewellery.

Their house belonged to a group of new builds at the edge of the village. It only took them moments to reach the fields and to skirt the Dyke. The paths were in full sun. A sweat drenching sun, even at 5 pm. The tracks were as hard as tarmac, their footsteps bouncing off the dry earth like tennis balls on a clay court.

They didn't stop at the first woodland that they reached. That was too close to home – it was just on the edge of Dyke territory and kids fed up with the tyre rope swing had been known to venture there. Instead, Jonny and Heather crossed over to another field and headed up the hill.

To the right of the field behind a low hedge, a large wooden pole towered. An orange wind-sock, the size of a flag, which was attached to the pole drifted lazily in the July heat; the hot movement of air – you could hardly call it a breeze – occasionally making it rise and fall as if playing with a toy. Jonny made his way over to the hedge and peered through to the private landing field behind. It was empty – as usual. There were no planes to be seen, although he knew they landed and took off sometimes. He and Heather had seen them, but they had never seen the people who lived in the house or who owned the planes.

"Maybe nobody lives there?" Heather had said wide-eyed when they had first skirted the edge of the airfield and got as close to the house as they could. All the windows were shut and a pot of plants was drying out by the front door.

"Somebody does for sure," Jonny answered. "Or at least someone's visited – there are tyre marks on the drive."

"Could be the postman," she said with a shrug, losing interest. "Come on Jonny, race you to the den!"

Today, as they approached the hedge and, out of habit, peered through, they noticed that a window at the front of the house was open and a dog was barking from somewhere close by, possibly around the back of the house in the garden. But there were no planes, still no planes. Heather looked at Jonny questioning silently what he wanted to do.

"I'm hungry," he said. "Let's go to the den."

They had built their den in the woods parallel to the airfield. They had pulled branches from the woodland floor and laid them against the trunk of a tree creating a wigwam. It was a haphazard structure and likely to fall down, but it was cool inside. Jonny took off his backpack. His tee-shirt was damp where the bag had been adding extra heat to his flesh, so he took it off also and dropped it on the floor. Heather reached into the bag and took a swig of water from the water bottle that Jonny had put in the bag earlier, before passing it to him to drink from.

"What are you going to do?" she asked her brother.

"I brought my pen-knife. I'm going to cut back some twigs for the den walls, then I'm going to eat my tea," he answered.

"A door would be more useful."

"Alright, make a door then."

"Can't. Don't have a knife."

"Pity."

"Can't I use yours?"

"No. I'll be using it."

"Pig! What's the point in having a brother?"

A low grumble grew in the sky. They almost missed it with their bickering. The grumble achieved a more perfect silence in the siblings than their mother had ever done.

"The aeroplane," Heather mouthed, her brown eyes saucers in her tanned skin.

"Quick," Jonny commanded and he shoved Heather out of the den. They ran, scrambling, to the edge of their wood and on, to the side of the airfield.

They were just in time to see a light aircraft approach over the field that they had crossed earlier. In seconds it had descended, touching down in the private airfield, where it taxied close to the house, alongside which stood a hangar, and drew to a halt.

~ Hugging the edge of the wood and keeping close to the ground, Jonny and Heather crept as close as they dared to the plane.

A man in canvas shorts, a white shirt and a navy baseball cap got down from the plane. He turned round to receive a large shape, covered in what appeared to be a blanket, thrust at him from the plane's interior, quickly followed by another man wearing jeans and a bomber jacket despite the heat.

"Attention! Sois-prudent!"

"Je fais ce que je peux et je n'ai pas besoin de ton aide."

The voices faded as the two men bundled the blanketed shape into the house where a woman stood at the open door, firmly shutting it behind the new arrivals when they had crossed the threshold.

"What was that all about?" Jonny asked.

"Suspicious," Heather replied.

"Definitely."

The children watched for a few more minutes but became bored when there was no further stir from the house or the airfield – not even the barking of the dog.

It was late when they decided to go home; it was beginning to get dark. The heat was still exhausting. Jonny thought about asking Mum if he could sleep outside in the small back garden. She'd have a fit if he suggested the wood and in any case, he wasn't in any hurry to tell her about their den.

"Where've you been?" she asked them when they let themselves in through the front door, Heather not bothering to take the ribbon off from her neck, so her head seemed to be involved in the unlocking operation.

"Just playing," Heather replied and then added, "thanks for tea."

"Yeah thanks, Mum, we ate out in the field." It was sort of the truth.

The next morning was a little cooler and Jonny rose early for his paper round before school. He met Dan at the end of his road and they headed together on their bikes to the corner shop to begin the job of stuffing the papers into their large shoulder bags in the order in which they would be delivered. At fourteen Jonny wasn't much bothered by the headlines but today was different. Splashed across each front page was the smiling photograph of Peter Morrisey the record-breaking British runner who was on the verge of a large medal haul at the Olympics in Montreal. On the verge of, not guaranteed, because he had disappeared – vanished overnight.

This was big news, important news. Dan scoured the articles as Jonny filled their bags for their rounds

"It says here it must be the Russians."

"Why the Russians?"

"Because they want to win all the medals – they take out their opponents."

"What by bumping them off?"

"He might not be dead. They might just have, you know, hidden him somewhere."

Jonny completed his round in unusual silence, thinking about Peter Morrisey and the Russians.

When he got back home Heather had already left for school; she liked to be early and chat with her friends first. He thought about scoffing his breakfast to try and catch up with her to tell her about the headline news, but there wasn't any point trying to speak to her at school, as he knew she would cut him dead, ignoring him in front of her friends. They both did. He'd have to wait until they were back at home that afternoon he thought, slurping the milk, no longer fridge-chilled, around his cornflakes warming with the day.

School was boring. The classrooms were hot and stuffy. He didn't want to be there. It was the perfect environment for the cold war plot to take hold in his head and to grow.

"You see it's got to be the Russians," he said in a low voice to Heather. Mum was upstairs in her bedroom putting on her uniform ready to go to her night shift at the hospital and he didn't want her to hear.

Heather pulled a face, she wasn't convinced.

"They were talking a funny language," he urged. "It had to be Russian."

"I don't know," Heather said doubtfully. "I thought Russian sounded more like a cassette being played backwards, kind of all stretched out."

"And they had someone in the plane, Heather, someone they didn't want anyone to see. It was a man, definitely a man, covered in a blanket."

Heather had to admit she had seen the same thing and it was all very strange.

"I think we should go and find out," Jonny said.

"But if they're Russians and if they've kidnapped Morrisey, they could be dangerous."

"We won't get caught, Heather. We'll just take a look and then tell the police."

The children waited for Mum to leave and then waited to eat their tea. Then they waited a little bit more for the day to become as dusky as they dared. They hurried through the fields to the airfield. The orange windsock looked grey in the night daylight. The house appeared to be empty. There were no planes in the field. Jonny and Heather crept up to the hangar. It was a wooden barn-like structure with a lock on the large double doors. The children placed their eyes against the cracks in the planks of wood, straining to see what could be inside.

All of a sudden, a dog started barking, it was in the garden behind them. A torch shone brightly in their faces.

"Merde! Qu'est-ce que vous faîtes là?" a Russian voice growled.

"Run," Heather shrieked, and she grabbed Jonny by the hand and yanked him away from the hanger door.

"Arrêtez," the voice shouted. The dog in front of the man barked loudly, straining on its lead.

Jonny needed no encouragement. The two scrambled wildly along the track to the wood and fled through the field back to the edge of the Dyke, convinced the dog was on their trail, that the Russians were pursuing them.

The Dyke was full of darkness. The canopy of the trees, so welcome during the hot recent days, formed a night-time tunnel through which the children ran blindly, trusting to their instinct. When they reached their front doorstep they felt like thieves breaking into their own home, the house was so silent and still.

"Are we safe?" Heather asked her older brother with trembling lips.

Jonny took deep gulps of air, drawing oxygen into his lungs, to recover from his escape. There was no way he was a Peter Morrisey.

"Yeah, they couldn't have followed, not through the Dyke," he answered his sister.

"What are we going to do now?"

Jonny thought for a moment, considering their best options.

"See what's in the fridge and then go to bed," was his response.

Honestly, brothers! Heather thought. But not coming up with a better plan herself she complied. She wasn't really sure it had sounded like Russian anyway.

4.
BUNYAN'S COTTAGE

The traveller clutched his cloak tight to his breast to keep the thick wind at bay and continued his purpose through the quiet lanes from Whitwell to Kimpton and then on to Wheathampstead. Eyes to the ground, he picked his path through the winter mud where puddles irrigated streams so that his sodden toes should not become more so. He carried a bundle tied fast over his shoulder. A large black felt hat sheltered his white-whiskered face from the rain. A bedraggled crow, the old preacher trudged, determinedly on.

He had taken his luncheon at a public house at Kimpton, a simple meal of bread, cheese and apple cake. There they had pressed him to tarry longer, to enjoy their hospitality, to rest in a comfortable inn-bed for the night; an old man like him should not walk what remained of his way from Bedford. No, Joseph Lambert, the tinker would be journeying to St Albans on the morrow and would convey him. But the late November sky was darkening and daylight hours remained few. Furthermore, he had a reason for returning to Wheathampstead this day.

"Master Bunyan, you are soaked through," Mistress Coleman greeted him in distress at his appearance as she opened the cottage door. "Come quickly, brother, and warm yourself by the fire. Jonathan, run and bid your father come. Tell him that Master Bunyan has arrived and then go and waken your grandfather."

The child rose from the settle positioned at a right-angle from the glowing fire. The honoured guest, he knew, would be offered the warmest seat on the settle, the one nearest to the flames. So he placed his book down carefully in the space beside that place, hoping that the great man would notice it, before leaving the room to do as his mother had bid.

With the bustle of a mother hen, Martha Coleman ushered the preacher to her fireside, lightening him of his mud-splattered cloak and furnishing him with a warming bowl of broth.

"Thank you kindly, sister Martha," Bunyan smiled across his broad cheekbones, and stretched his old limbs cat-like by the hearth as the wood flames began to thaw his chilled veins.

He picked up the book left pointedly by his side. It was a copy of his Dream, his allegory of the Christian journey, his *Pilgrim's Progress*. Not a first edition but certainly an early copy, likely six years old, the well-worn edges of the thick crisp paper making it seem older.

"His grandfather taught him to read with that book," Martha explained.

"It is certainly well worn."

"Oh Master Bunyan, if you could only know what your book means to us," Martha burst, a moment of passion flying up like a spark from low embers.

"It is the Lord to whom you should give thanks, not I."

He was still unaccustomed to the enthusiastic praises from friends and strangers and answered abruptly. Too abruptly. The light in the woman was quenched by the rebuke.

"But thank you, never-the-less, sister Martha, and I am pleased that Jonathan studies the Dream."

"I do, sir," Jonathan's breaking voice reappeared by the settle, having completed his task, claiming his right to respond on his behalf in his mother's conversation.

The old man looked fondly at the grandson of one of his dearest friends.

"Jonathan, would you tell an old preacher such as I, what your burden might be and what shape your castle might take?"

His mother busied herself with the meal so as not to hear her son's confession whilst keeping an ear to his words.

Jonathan crept close to the great preacher.

"My burden, sir, is the path my family would have me take. My castle…"

"Master Bunyan," his father interrupted, joyfully entering the room, "you are most welcome!"

Behind his father a sound shuffled – Robert Coleman, the grandfather, aged, hunched, blue eyes bleared by growing cataracts and sleep cut short.

"John," the old man said softly.

"Robert," the preacher replied, beckoning him to the settle by the fire where they embraced, old friends, and sat in wordless companionship, two old men staring into the golden flames.

In the fire's light, they saw themselves young again, not two, but three: John Bunyan, Robert Coleman and John Fowler. Three young men in their prime, fervent, devout and full of vigour.

The eve had been chill that September. Beech leaves were beiging. Already a crowd was gathering on the green outside the cottage: farmers, tinkers, traders, young, old, husbands, wives, children all assembled on the grass common land. Becloaked and expectant, their hushed conversations rose like a soft wind and crept around the doorframes, the window frames and the cracks of the cottage to the three men inside.

Bunyan, smartly dressed in black, waited by the hearth, taut like a spring expecting its release, an actor standing in the wings of the stage listening for his cue.

"We will soon be ready," John Fowler, the oldest of the three, detailed. "Adam Long is keeping watch out on Green Lane, Michael Turner is at Beech Hyde and will be quick to warn of disturbance. Robert, you have identified the leaders to show the paths from Symondshyde wood should we all need to leave in haste?"

Robert Coleman nodded.

"From whence do they come?" Bunyan asked.

"From all around – Wheathampstead, Sandridge, Welwyn, St Albans," Fowler responded.

"That is too wide, brother," Coleman worried. "Surely a secret spread that far is no more a secret?"

"And so we have a plan," Fowler asserted firmly.

"The word of our Lord cannot be kept silent," determined Bunyan. "We will trust to His will and His care – and be cautious."

A small boy watched the three in awe from his hiding place behind the settle. He followed them, a miniature shadow, as they left the cottage.

When Bunyon had appeared on the green, a wave of hush had rolled across the assembly, like a soft gust of wind stroking the tips of the surrounding beech wood.

"Brothers, sisters," Bunyan began, "Our risen Lord is here with us …."

The boy crouched low at his mother's side, drinking in the preacher's words, the truth of the Word of God revealed to him by this devout man in black whose voice carried over the Green in the September stillness. A voice that carried words of encouragement and exhortation to a Bible faith that was simpler and purer than the faith of the established Church of England. He saw faces intent, eyes lifted, the discouraged encouraged, the troubled calmed.

Meanwhile, his father, Robert Coleman, stood guard at his vantage point outside the cottage where he could act instantly on a warning received from Adam Long down the lane and with a view the length of the Green to the Beech Hyde Road from whence the alarm could be raised by Michael Turner.

"Too many brethren," he thought fretfully, counting the flock. Five dozen – too many.

The preacher was concluding his sermon, urged on by the darkening of day, aware that some of his flock had several miles to return on foot to their beds, when suddenly Alan Long ran, breathless, fuelled by fear:

"They come – from Wheathampstead – the Militia!"

"Disperse!" Fowler commanded instantly.

Five dozen fearful Brethren fled silently, ushered quickly through to Symondshyde Wood from there to find paths in the directions of their homes taking circuitous tracks to be far from Coleman Green if they were waylaid.

"Goodbye, Robert. God be with you," Bunyan had blessed as Fowler pulled him into the ditch that ran behind the cottage – a ditch that became a stream – that lead to the river and took them away from the marching feet of the Militia.

Leaving Robert at the cottage on Coleman Green to pay the penalty.

The golden flames licked the wood that Martha had placed in the fireplace and the smoke hurried up and out of the cottage's chimney. Robert Coleman and his old friend

John Bunyan watched flame devour wood silently from their place on the settle, words hardly needed in their life-long friendship. Coleman's son, the watchful boy, now a man and father himself, stoked the fire with another log.

"He wrote that he would be travelling from London today. He will soon be here." Old Coleman said quietly.

All of their lives had taken different paths since that illegal religious gathering on the Green outside Robert Coleman's cottage in September 1660. How could they forget that date, the last time the friends had been together? Twenty-six years had passed and they had not seen John Fowler since and now tonight he would return. John Fowler – strong, decisive, ambitious.

Old Coleman lit his pipe and puffed thoughtfully,

"Can you think what brings him home after all this time? There has been no danger, not for these past eight years, not since you left Bedford gaol."

Bunyon shook his head. John Fowler, the only one of the three not to have been imprisoned for their faith, for their ideals, for their determination to live their lives as God demands, for their refusal to conform to the dictates of the Church of England. John Fowler, who had fled to Amsterdam in the autumn of 1660, when Bunyon was imprisoned at Bedford and Coleman at St Albans.

And then there were three. He had arrived. He was staying at The Sun Inn at Wheathampstead. How pleased he was to see his friends after all this time. Why didn't they eat then talk? The same Fowler, the same decisiveness, but a frailer man, his inadequate heart written clearly on his wrinkled flesh. For all his desire for a repast he ate but little. At the end of the meal, he said to his friends thoughtfully,

"I need to know that you do not hold it against me that I left."

"Why should we?" Old Robert Coleman asked.

"I worked hard in Amsterdam. There I am now a man of wealth and standing. I often contemplate the journey that my life might have taken if I had stayed in England that autumn. Would I have seen the inside of a gaol like you, my brothers? Would I have paid the price for my faith quietly or publicly?"

"God has given us all different paths, it is for us to live them according to His will," the old preacher replied wisely.

"And so I have John, so I believe I have. I worked and traded. When I learned of your *Pilgrim's Progress* I pressed for a Dutch translation and paid the costs of publication. I have done the same elsewhere wherever my trading connections have allowed. You can see with your own eyes that I will soon reach the Valley of the Shadow. I would not turn my eyes to face the Celestial City and hope for admittance without once more seeing my friends and asking for their pardon."

Coleman looked to Bunyon for leadership. He had resented Fowler's abandonment of their cause and over the years he had much regretted the loss of their friendship.

"There is nothing to pardon, my brother," John Bunyan said, quietly reaching for his friend's hand. Robert Coleman hesitated and then did the same. Fowler took the hands of the friends of his youth with a grateful heart and silent thanks.

"Robert," he said breaking the stillness, "I feel that in some small way I have assisted John from afar, but I have not had the opportunity to assist you."

"There is no need, I am perfectly content," Robert replied. "I am looked after in my old age in my home by my son and his wife. I have their love and that of my grandson."

Bunyon watched Jonathan reading at the kitchen table by candlelight.

"Jonathan," he called over to the boy. "A little earlier this evening you were telling me about your burden. Tell me, young man, what is your castle?" the Old Preacher asked.

Jonathan glanced nervously in his parents' direction, feeling awkward under the gaze of the unfamiliar merchant from Amsterdam.

"My parents expect me to farm as they have done, as Grandfather did. But that is not what I would wish for my path." He paused momentarily before gaining pace. "My wish would be to own a printing press and print books – your books, Master Bunyan, your sermons. I would wish to print books so that other children might learn to read and understand your *Pilgrim's Progress* for themselves as I can and as I have done." The child's face grew radiant in the fireside light as he explained his dream, his vision.

Throughout the boy's speech, John Fowler sat quietly, turning his pipe in his hand, turning it about, never raising it to his lips.

"Do you know where you might be apprenticed, Jonathan?" he asked.

"There is a printing press at St Albans, at the Abbey Gateway," the boy replied quickly sensing the wind was beginning to blow a favourable course.

"To my mind, that would be a fitting Christian path," affirmed the Old Preacher.

Fowler nodded. There would be much to do and much to fund from his purse. Jonathan's journey would extend for many years. The winds of change would blow through this cottage if Fowler took action.

"Riches stored on earth cannot be used in heaven," the old trader commented.

And John Bunyan, Robert Coleman, and John Fowler looked from one to the other in agreement. Three elderly puritans reunited by the fireside in the cottage on Coleman green.

5.
THE COMMON OF ADVENTURE

Mary wriggled on the sweaty bus leather seat, blonde curls damp with perspiration. The August sun shining in through the glass was making her hot and uncomfortable. It was still a long time until lunch but all she could think about was the picnic inside the hamper that her cousin Margaret was holding tightly on her lap. It would be a feast, no doubt. There would be cheese sandwiches and apples for sure and oh please, please let there be the scones that she had smelt baking that morning – perhaps with a slim spreading of strawberry jam, please let Aunt Helen have packed them as a treat. She had not dared to ask. It was not polite to ask about food.

Her older brother Jonathan sat on the seats behind them next to their cousin Shirley, Margaret's younger sister. His face was a thunder cloud.

"I don't see why I had to come with you lot," he grumbled.

"Mother would not have let you come to Nomansland Common by yourself," Margaret lectured. She was in charge today and it would be no bad thing, in her view, if Jonathan was reminded of that fact. "You'll have to stay with us when we get there and you mustn't go off by yourself."

"Our mother lets me do all kinds of things by myself, doesn't she, Mary?" he turned to his little sister to corroborate his statement of independence. "And I'm in the

Scouts. I learned how to help the Fire Wardens if there was a raid."

"But you're on holiday with my mother and father, and Mother says you have to stay with us," Margaret reminded him.

Jonathan sat back in his seat fuming that his cousin Margaret was such a goody-goody, telling him what he should and shouldn't do. He didn't want to be out today with his cousins or his little sister. He just wanted to be alone.

"I like coming out together like this," Shirley said, trying to bring some peace to the troubled waters on the bus. "It's like going on an adventure."

An Adventure. Mary closed her eyes and imagined Noman's Land Common. An island in the middle of a wide river of warm swirling silver mist which only children could cross in gondolas of gold. An Island where all manner of delicacies would grow, like bananas, chocolate, Turkish Delight! She could just about remember bananas from before the war. She'd been a very little girl when the war had broken out but she could still remember bananas, bananas, and custard 'delish!' Chocolate she had tasted occasionally but Turkish Delight she'd only read about – rich, exotic, perfumed, foreign – fitting for an adventure. And on the island, the children would be looked after by beautiful medieval damsels dressed in flowing silk gowns, guardians who were never cross or told you it was not polite to ask questions about what was for lunch or dinner.

"Oh dear!" the little dreamer exclaimed with a sharp intake of breath, her eyes wide beneath their thick spectacle lenses – a new idea worrying her.

"Margaret, why is it called Noman's Land?" that not-to-be spoken place belonging to the First World War, a word in a shadowy language scarcely whispered, events hushed over by parents' "don't ask questions."

No nonsense Margaret, fourteen years old and so grown up, in charge of the party, in charge of the picnic, smiled at her little cousin and explained in her most teacherly way,

"A long time ago the Bishop of St Albans owned all the land on one side of the common and the Bishop of Westminster owned all the land on the other, but they couldn't agree who owned the common in between, it was said to belong to neither – to 'No Man,'" she explained.

"They rowed for – oh ever such a long time," Shirley interrupted, " – and in the end, a jury sorted it out for them and put a piece of Hertfordshire Puddingstone in the middle to mark as the boundary. We can go and look for it if you like when we get there."

Pudding Stone – that sounded like something to look forward to Mary thought.

"You didn't think Nomansland was to do with the Trenches did you?" scoffed Jonathan. "You are a silly little girl."

A tear welled up behind Mary's thick spectacles and threatened to plop from her face onto her bare knees which could not be covered up by her slightly too small sundress. A dress that needed to last the rest of the summer, since her mother was saving her ration coupons for a larger, winter one.

"Why does Jonathan have to be so beastly to me?" Mary thought as the bus bumped along the road to the common. He used to be so much fun to be with, playing with her and kind when she made mistakes because she was simply younger than he was, but now he was horrible.

"Nomansland Common next stop" the bus driver called and Margaret had to scramble to make sure all four children and the picnic descended safely at the bus stop on the road from Sandridge, which ran the side-length of the common.

Nomansland Common – an Adventure. Jonathan surveyed the landscape neatly cut in two by a country lane. To the left scrubland – August drying grass, scratchy gorse, the remnants of unsuccessful crops grown on too-thin soil by German and Italian PoWs. To his right a different country – the lush green carpet of a quintessentially English cricket ground. He was in luck, he could see figures in white on the pitch. If he hurried, he might watch some play.

He set off without consulting his cousins.

"Jonathan, Mother said we must stay together," Margaret called after him crossly. That boy was such a nuisance, he'd only been staying with them for a few days, but she couldn't wait for him to go home. Mary was sweet though. Mary could stay.

"He doesn't want to be with us," Mary said sadly.

Jonathan strode off. No, he did not want to be with a bunch of silly girls. What did they know about cricket? About how important this ground was? Matches here since the early 1800s, maybe earlier and Apsley Cherry Garrard one of the youngest members of the British Antarctic Expedition led by Captain Scott played a match here just before he left for that ill-fated journey to the Pole. Now that was an adventure. A real adventure. Jonathan stored the nugget of information carefully. Such nuggets of knowledge would be important to help him when he started at his new boarding school in September. Each day the new term was getting closer. Each day his worries about what it would be like, whether he would fit in, would he make new friends, would the work be too hard? clenched his throat and tried to strangle him.

"Never mind him – come on, Mary, I'll show you the common."

Shirley pulled her little cousin up the hill whilst Margaret tut-tutted in a grown-up sort of way with her eyes still on Jonathan.

Nomansland Common – An adventure. It didn't matter how many times Shirley had come here, she always felt her heart swell with the romance of the barren landscape, the land of Katherine Ferrers the Highway Woman. And soon there was going to be a picture all about her, Mummy had said. *The Wicked Lady* was to be released in the autumn starring Margaret Lockwood. "Oh please Mummy, please may I see it," Shirley had begged wide-eyed. But Mummy wasn't sure. Maybe she and Daddy would treat themselves to a showing at the picture house first to see if it were suitable for a child.

Margaret Lockwood as Katherine Ferrers. How perfectly thrilling! The Hertfordshire Highwaywoman, who terrorised the travellers on the common. "Your money or your life!" she would cry as she stole jewels, laced silk handkerchiefs and purses of gold on the road that she, Shirley, had just travelled by bus. How exciting that she shared the footsteps of the romantic heroine. How deliciously shocking that a woman could be a heroine and bad. Shirley couldn't wait for November.

Margaret followed the girls slowly up the hill, hamper in hand. That horrid boy couldn't get too lost and anyway she was the one carrying the food so he would surely find them, like a hunting terrier sniffing out his lunch. The younger girls would romanticise about the Wicked Lady, if she knew Shirley, and there was the Puddingstone to occupy them too. On balance, Margaret reflected, she could lay aside her mantle of adult responsibility and enjoy herself until lunchtime.

What a place the common was – flint heads from four thousand years BC had been discovered here, cannonballs from the Wars of the Roses dug out of the ground. If the buckle were to fall from her shabby brown shoe and if she or some other person were to tread it into the ground, the buckle would lie here undiscovered through the centuries until someone in the future would find it here on the common. Someone from the future, maybe having a picnic.

But would people of the future eat picnics? Margaret turned the historical and the philosophical around in her head.

She nearly trod on it, so lost in thought she was, she nearly trod on it, like the imaginary lost buckle. Margaret bent down and picked it up. A well-worn brown leather wallet separated from its owner. She looked up and around quickly, not a person in sight other than Shirley and Mary a little way ahead. Someone must have dropped it, what a bother for them.

What should she do? Should she look inside? But it was private. It would be like snooping in someone's drawers or prying inside other people's envelopes of post. Feeling very sensible, she decided to make her camp where she was, despite the lack of shade on the open common and wait for the owner of the wallet to find her with it.

"…and if you put the puddingstone at the entrance to your house it will keep the witches away."

"Witches?" mouthed Mary.

"Yes. They steal babies and handkerchiefs," Shirley explained knowingly.

"Did people used to try and eat the stone to keep the witches away?"

"No – that's garlic and vampires. This stone is bad for your teeth. But it does look like Christmas pudding before it's cooked with all the raisins and dried fruit mixed in, don't you think?"

It was true. It did look like a fruit pudding.

"I'm hungry," Mary announced.

It wasn't long before the three girls were sitting happily down in the sunshine munching on their picnic which contained – oh joy of joys, scones with strawberry jam. Jonathan, the hunting terrier, bounded up the hill and threw himself down on the ground alongside the picnic.

"What's that?" he asked pointing at the wallet.

"It's a wallet" Margaret replied.

"I can see that."

"I found it."

"Whose is it?"

"I don't know."

"Well haven't you looked inside?" Goodness, how brainless girls could be!

Jonathan snatched the wallet from Margaret's hand and looked inside before she could protest. Two small photos; one of a lady in a WAAC uniform and another of a little cottage with honeysuckle growing around the door, a miniature embroidered Union Jack, a rabbit's foot, a hankie with the initials J.P, two one-pound notes and, ah that was more like it, a driving licence and identity papers for a James Payne.

"We must get all this back to him," Jonathan declared decidedly.

"I know that!" Margaret was irritated. "I've been sitting here with it for at least half an hour now in case he retraces his steps."

"I've got a better idea than sitting here. There's a hotel next to the cricket ground let's take the wallet there when we've had our lunch," he said, helping himself to a cheese sandwich from the hamper which he devoured as if he hadn't been fed for more than a month.

The landlord of the Park Hotel looked up from the bar where he had spread today's paper. He had been frightfully disturbed during the morning so had hardly read more than the headlines before the lunchtime rush. Now that it was quieter, he intended to finish. He stroked the two sides of his dark moustache with his thumb and forefinger rhythmically as he read.

"No children in the bar," he scowled at the sight of Margaret, Jonathan, Shirley, and Mary.

"Excuse me, sir," launched Jonathan in his most polite tone of voice. "We found this wallet on the common and thought it best if we brought it here."

"Well let's see it, young man."

"It belongs to a James Payne," Margaret interrupted with eyebrows raised to Jonathan to prevent him from handing over the wallet too soon.

"Never heard of him," the landlord frowned.

"Yes you have, love," the landlord's wife breezed in. "Gunner Jim – you know!" and turning to the children explained, "He often stays here, on account of Jessie-May in the village," and then with a large smile, "why don't you sit outside the front in the shade and I'll bring you some lemonade – the bar's not the place for youngsters, then you can give him the wallet when he gets back, he won't be long."

Lemonade! Marvellous!

The children were savouring the last drops of the cool sweet lemon when Gunner Jim, in civies, returned agitated by the loss of his wallet and accompanied by Jessie-May, also not in uniform now but a navy polka dot wrap dress. Needless to say, he was delighted to be reunited with his wallet and its contents. In a broad Yorkshire accent, he ordered another round of lemonade for the children with a thick slice of sweet sticky Lazy Daisy cake for each of them.

Gunner Jim did not look like a soldier, but neither did many of those recently demobilised. He turned out to be a jolly good chap though. He had crossed the channel to France on D-Day and had heaved a giant gun across Europe. Soon he would be going home to Yorkshire where he would play county cricket and Jessie-May would be going with him as his wife. Jonathan ate the details up. Shirley swooned at the romance.

"That was a first-class afternoon, Captain Margaret," Jonathan, sweetened by an unusual amount of sugar and cricket, admitted, as the bus approached from Wheathampstead village to take the cousins home to St Albans. "I'll carry the hamper for you," he added.

Margaret wasn't sure if his gesture was an apology or an attempt to see if there were any more sandwiches left in the wicker basket. Either way, it was a white flag, of sorts.

"Thank you," she said, passing him the hamper.

He took it from Margaret in one hand and with the other, he helped Mary, who was tired and sleepy, onto the bus, and sat her down next to him. She snuggled into the side of her big brother and he put his arm around her.

Two glasses of lemonade, scones with jam, Lazy Daisy cake, a missing wallet, a wartime romance, a kind big brother, a handkerchief collecting Highway Woman, witches eating Christmas Pudding stone and trees blossoming with Turkish Delight on an Island where only children were allowed, swirled around Mary's head as, grubby and contented, she fell asleep on the bus on the way home from her Common of Adventure, sugar sticking to her damp blonde curls.

6.

HEARTWOOD

Quietly, Linden stepped out of his home in the middle of the ancient woodland. He could smell the excitement on the air, he could stretch out and feel the electric pulse of expectancy. The summer evening was humid, a thunderstorm was brewing. There was no time to waste, all must be completed before the rain came. He reached back inside his home and pulled out two woven mats made from heart-shaped leaves and placed them carefully at the threshold of his dwelling.

Hazel was first to arrive, startling him with her light footsteps on the woodland floor.

"Linden, it has been too long," she breezed with a papery kiss.

"Time passes," he whispered in reply.

It had been forty years since the King and Queen had last called upon him to convene a council. Forty summers ago their collective fear, fuelled by skies filled with fire, had been very great. The smell of burning and sounds of desperation which carried across the counties on the wind, night after night, had terrified their tranquillity. What atrocities were happening in the world of humans? They had convened in urgency, but could not fathom it. Eventually, the skies had quietened and peace returned to their world.

A rustling, and Hornbeam was there.

"Good evening," his double bass voice echoed in the stillness as he took his place next to Hazel to be joined in moments by Holly, Birch, Ash, Elm, Hawthorne and Rowan, greeting each other warmly and politely, creating a circle beneath the great lime of the ancient wood. They waited in the evening stillness, listening to the beating of gnats wings, the pitter-patter of caterpillar feet, the swelling of growing nuts. Into the natural peace, King Oak and Queen Beech processed. King Oak – ancient, authoritative, cloaked in rich dark green. Queen Beech – beautiful, charismatic, dressed in shimmering shades of copper. The monarchs took their places on the heartleaf mats. The council had begun.

A tiny brown mouse sniffed at the base of a birch standing sentinel at the borders of the council ring. His little nose twitched, as he smelled the thick, sweet perfume of the Tree Spirits. Each was a pillar of a unique scent. A scent that was green and moist. A scent that was physical and solid. With his beady eyes, Mr Mouse looked closer. Of course he knew who they were. He knew their fragrance and the murmur of their voices, the distinct, subtle tones of rustling oak, rustling birch, rustling holly. But he had never seen them and nor had his father or his father's father. He crept soundlessly to the edge of the circle. All were seated except one. Tall and strong the one stood, his core column of scent covered in green heart-shaped leaves that rearranged themselves with a flutter into arms or legs or fingers or whatever form Linden needed his spirit self to take a thought to action. Closest to little Mouse sat Hawthorne – a bride in a flounced gown of snowy blossom. Next to her was Rowan his dark green suit decorated with clusters of scarlet berries glinting in the late evening sunshine. Mr Mouse savoured every detail of the tree council to tell his children and his children's children.

Linden, the convenor, began:

"Friends, their Majesties King Oak and Queen Beech have called us here today because a great crisis is upon us. The seasons are changing. Rain drenches us leaving our roots waterlogged in winter, whilst in summer droughts bring thirst. Each of us has observed how spring arrives earlier than of yore to waken our friends the bees from their winter sleep, only to trick them with renewed snaps of cold and the promise of a larder of nectar from flowers not yet in bloom."

"It is true," Hornbeam continued. "I have lived in this woodland for three hundred years. When I was a sapling the air was pure, the raindrops clean, the soil delicious. But now that which feeds me tastes noxious and bitter."

"But what is it? What is happening to us?" Birch asked in a whisper laden with anxiety.

"We do not know." Linden shook his leaves sadly as he spoke.

"Can mankind help?" piped Holly.

"Mankind!" King Oak snorted from his seat of honour. "Man who used to venerate this woodland. Man, who in my youth respected us, taking only from us what was needed for his livelihood and well-being." As he spoke his green leaves bristled in indignation and regret. "Man cannot be trusted."

The Tree Spirits rustled their scented forms into arms which reached out to the Spirit on either side in a circular base of solidarity, committed to standing together as one against the poorly understood danger.

"There is hope," Queen Beech gently voiced into the circle. "A child, a Tree Whisperer."

"A Tree Whisperer, Whisperer, Whisperer," the circle echoed.

"They are few my dear. What say you, Linden?"

Linden gave space to the humid silence as he thought. He was hundreds of years old, like his fellow Tree Spirits. So many from the race of mankind had passed through the woodland in his lifetime. When he was young they took wood for their fires, to make their tools, their buildings, they sought leaves and bark for their medicines. Later, men had trampled the woods with their guns to shoot, kill and hunt. In recent times folk came walking with dogs, with families, with picnics. King Oak was right, where once the trees had been venerated, of late they were admired by some for an external beauty but mostly they were ignored, their importance denied. Was it possible to call a Tree Whisperer?

"It seems to me your Majesties, that we must trust to hope. We must try to call a Tree Whisperer."

Oak, Beech, Lime, Hornbeam, Hazel, Elm, Ash, Birch, Hawthorne and Holly nodded in agreement and rustling their leaves sending a wave of sound like a deep crash from their epicentre out through the ancient wood. A Tree Whisperer would be called. And with that declaration the storm began, drenching the canopy, soaking the ground below. Little Mouse scampered quickly to his dry nest to tell the tale.

The Tree Spirits returned to their tree homes throughout the woodland and watched and waited. They sent news of sightings to each other through their network of underground roots. They issued messages of possibilities coded in scents and born on the breeze.

One September evening a troop of young boys brought by their adults entered the woodland. In blue jeans and green sweaters with gold neckties, they looked like a flock of fledgling woodpeckers. The boys ran happily through the trees collecting sticks, acorns and leaves, obeying and disobeying their adults by turn in a romp of an adventure. All but one little lad, who trod carefully over the roots and looked with seeing eyes around him.

Linden knew this was the one. He called to the boy in his beautiful lime voice and with his sweet lime scent. He whispered to the child's soul and the child answered.

Charlie Brookes, without ever knowing how, found himself standing before an immense tree on the cub evening expedition to the old wood to gain the nature badge. He had been so excited about the trip. He loved being outside. His mother laughed at how he would rather study bugs than fractions, leaves than nouns. Most of his childhood was a happy blur but he would never, all his life, forget what it was like to stand before the lime tree.

He knew that the tree was old, that it was great, that it was special. He remembered reaching out and touching the rough bark and feeling a pulse of energy move through him as suddenly he knew what he wanted to be – not an astronaut or a train driver, not even a vet – he wanted to be a man who cared for trees.

"I will," Charlie whispered. "I will look after you."

And to seal the promise Linden let flutter a heart shape leaf which Charlie caught and put safely in his jeans pocket.

Charlie Brookes returned frequently to the old wood as he turned from a child to a teen to a man. Unknowingly and full of respect, he met each of the tree spirits in turn. The years passed, a new century dawned and Charlie was ready to act.

"So what's your new job, mate?" Harry questioned, taking a sip of his lager in The Wicked Lady on the edge of Nomansland Common at Wheathampstead where they all met on a Friday night.

"Site Manager of Heartwood," Charlie smiled with modest pleasure.

"Heartwood?" questioned Yvonne, opening a packet of salt and vinegar crisps with difficulty, accidentally tearing the packet so that the crisps spilt out over the table.

"You know the old wood near Sandridge where we used to play when we were kids? Well, it's one of the oldest woods in England. The plan is to plant a new wood with native species and then the two will one day join up to form the largest new native forest in the country. The new wood is Heartwood."

"Heart wood because you love it?" Harry teased.

"No, heart because that's the shape of the old lime tree's leaf," Julie defended, helping herself to some of Yvonne's spilt crisps.

"But mate, you used to be all 'climate change this' and 'climate change that' how will a wood help?"

Yvonne rolled her eyes and smiled weakly at Julie who raised a sympathetic eyebrow in return.

Charlie thought for a moment,

"You're right," he said leaning forward, "it's easy to be evangelical when you're a student," (Julie wondered if Harry knew what the word 'evangelical' meant) "but honestly this is a great job. We're going to plant thousands of trees. That will help fight climate change. And the planting will attract wildflowers and insects. Then eventually the two woods will merge, all kinds of birds will find new habitats. It's going to be great!" And he leaned back in his chair, eyes shining, and took another sip of his pint.

"What, plant them all by yourself?" Harry guffawed, looking at the girls to back him in his teasing.

"Actually Harry, I thought you and I would volunteer to help," Yvonne stated. Harry's face fell. He looked around at his friends' faces around the pub table: Yvonne adamant, Julie sceptical and Charlie pleased. He put his hands up in mock resignation,

"Alright, alright, I'll plant."

Charlie chuckled. "Don't worry it won't just be you. We're going to involve the whole community. We're going to get hordes of scouting groups – girls and boys, junior schools, to plant as well. You never know," he added cheekily, "if Yvonne's cooking a little boy in there maybe he'll be a cub like we were and plant too."

Yvonne looked pleased and Harry looked nervous.

"Typical," thought Julie as she reached for Charlie's hand under the table – wondering what their own cub would be like.

Linden stepped out of his lime tree home. He felt older, stiffer than before but his heart was light. Thirty years since the last council but now something had changed. Hazel and Hornbeam were the first to join the circle as before.

"We can all smell the saplings but they are not our progeny – where are they? How did they come to be near to us?" questioned King Oak.

"Your Majesty, the bees tell me that a great many humans of all sizes are planting on the other side of the ridge," Hawthorne explained quietly.

"Am I correct that each of you can smell your kin?" Linden queried.

Leaves rustled around the circle in the affirmative.

"A new wood!" Elm, incredulous, sighed softly on the edge of his breath.

"How will it help us?"

"Who is responsible?"

"How large will it be?"

Questions flurried in the air around the council circle. Questions seeking answers from Linden.

"Charlie Brookes, without a doubt," he declared. "As to the rest of your questions I cannot tell, but our Tree Whisperer is behind this and he will care for us."

"Well said," judged King Oak.

"Friends – we must welcome the young ones," Queen Beech commanded.

The council ended, the spirits returned to their homes and instructed their offspring in the ancient wood around them to yearn, to yearn with passion through their roots, through their leaf scent, and to call to the new baby trees to grow strong and healthy and meet the old wood soon.

Linden shook his heart-shaped leaves and wafted his lime tree scent onto the wind.

"Thank you, Charlie," he whispered.

"You're welcome," Charlie replied on the wind.

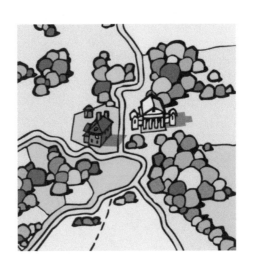

VILLAGES
AYOT ST LAWRENCE

7.
THE PALLADIAN CHURCH

Richard Corby, newly appointed ecclesiastical secretary to Thomas Thurlow, Bishop of Lincoln, rode his weary horse along the lane which lead from Wheathampstead to Codicote, and into the little village of Ayot St Lawrence. For the last six weeks, he had been conducting his first inspection, of what would become many, of the Bishop's Hertfordshire parishes and now he had arrived to undertake the visit which was likely to be the most distasteful of his tour. He declined refreshment from the landlord at 'The Three Horseshoes' deciding instead to make the most of the end of day October sunshine and see for his own eyes the problems that Sir Lionel Lyde had created for the Bishop, and by extension himself as the Bishop's representative. At twenty-five years of age, he had more energy and inclination to continue his day, than it seemed to him his horse had.

Corby stepped out from the timber-framed inn. He was purposeful and swift of foot. Within no more than a dozen steps he was standing before the church – a neglected, pitiful church. He opened the gate and entered the sacred grounds, passing the graves of villagers long dead. His eyes scanned the structure of the semi-ruin dedicated to the village's saint. The tower was crumbling, the roof of the nave appeared to have fallen in, large sections of the brickwork from the chancel were missing. He approached the entrance, but where he would have expected to find the heavy oak door, there was nothing more than an empty space into which the wind had blown a vegetal congregation of dry brown leaves.

He delved further into the dilapidated structure. Any church ornamentation which ought to have decorated the sacred interior had been removed. There was no longer any glass in the windows. There were no altar cloths, no candlesticks, no lectern, no wooden pulpit. His Secretary's eyes bore witness that the church had been emptied of all ephemera and that unlicenced hands were deconstructing the edifice, piece by piece.

Corby frowned and turned sharply clicking his heels in a way more reminiscent of a soldier than a secretary, but in some ways he was a soldier, the Bishop's soldier, fighting his prelate's cause in parishes far away.

Upon leaving the church, he spied an old lady on her hands and knees tending a grave in the shadows of an ancient yew.

"Good evening, mistress," he greeted with an amiable smile.

"Good evening, sir," she replied guardedly, eying the stranger with suspicion, not breaking off from her task in hand.

"I am sorry for your loss," he continued, alluding to the grave she tended, on which were inscribed the names of a father, a mother, a husband, and a son. She nodded silently and continued to weed the soil around the grave with a small fork.

"Your church is in need of repair," he commented.

"Some might say that, sir."

"I've heard the Baronet is building another church."

"You could say that, sir."

Corby was irritated by the old lady's lack of attention to his conversation, to his position, and clicked his heels together, leaning slightly forwards as he did so, considering whether to interrogate her further or to give her up as a loss.

She studied him carefully from the corner of her eye as she bent further across her grave to pull out a dandelion, depositing the useful leaves in the basket which she had alongside her. Strangers were not to be trusted, everyone knew that. Nor was it wise to say anything about the Baronet; in his favour or against, in support of his plans for the church or in disapproval of it.

Above their heads, a chorus of rooks cawed noisily in the trees and the sun, fast approaching its golden zenith, was casting long shadows across the graveyard.

Was this stranger not going to go away? Was he not going to leave her be? The heeled leather shoes and black stockings were still standing close. The man's body weight leaning forward as is if to pounce and then rocking back into its proper place, square on the soil, as if reconsidering, and had decided to wait a moment longer.

"Follow the path around Rose Cottage and you will see the new church, sir," she offered finally, hoping that this piece of information would see him on his way, which indeed it did.

Corby's route took him past the cottage where the last red roses of summer bloomed and into a field where cream, beige and black sheep grazed contentedly side by side. Ahead of him, across the field, white colonnades glowed pink in the October sunset.

"Good Lord!" Corby exclaimed, a shiver of delight and distaste running through his spine.

Here too it was as had been reported in the letters to Lincoln. The arrogant man had indeed completed what at first had been a rumour, and was now a Palladian fact. He had built himself a church in a field opposite his manor house. No new Parish church in the English tradition. Instead a collonaded Greek mausoleum. It was splendid. It was vile.

Corby made his way disbelievingly to the white temple blazing in the creamy-pink glory of the last rays of the afternoon sun. The church, more appropriate for the god Apollo than for the Almighty, occupied the centre of the edifice. To the right and to the left, colonnades reached out to touch two arched aedicula; a pair of shrines which could hardly be further apart from each other if they tried.

As he approached the steps of Sir Lyde's new church, Corby looked up and saw a tall lady who at that very instant was exiting the church through the blue-painted double doors beneath the portico. She glided, ghost-like, down the steps, an elegant goddess in dove grey silk and curled white wig. At first, she appeared not to notice him, but then without altering her features she said to the maid who followed her,

"The Secretary has arrived Susana."

The maid, unsure what she should make of this strange non-greeting to the handsome young man she had not seen before, replied hesitantly,

"Yes, milady."

As Rachel Lyde, wife of the Baronet, passed Corby on the steps, the fragrance of pressed rose petals drifted from the pomander she was carrying from her wrist and floated to his nostrils. She turned her white head back towards him before she left the church grounds to return across the field to the Manor House and called out,

"He will bury me one side and himself the other. We dine at 8 o'clock. We will expect you."

Corby watched entranced as the ghostlike figure and her maid floated across the field and entered the grounds of the Manor House, her rose fragrance lingering with him on the steps of the church. From where he stood, the manor appeared grand, impressive; as the new church would surely appear from the manor. There would be a particularly stunning view, he suspected, from the drawing-room, the Baronet's study, probably his private chambers too.

This Sir Lionel Lyde was an arrogant man. The source of his wealth? Well, who knew for sure. The tobacco plantations in the West Indies? Profiteering? Stocks and shares? The source of his land, however, was undisputed – a profitable marriage to his first cousin Rachel Lyde who had inherited the manor and its lands from her father, the Baronet's uncle. He was a man who did what he wanted, took from whoever he needed, and cared little for the consequence.

Standing on the steps of the new Greek Church, Corby clicked his heels in irritation. So far in his visit, he had discovered a church in purposeful ruins, an expensive monument which purported to be a place of worship and an invitation to dinner from the lady of the manor, old enough to be his mother and who smelt of roses.

He returned to the inn where he agreed now to some light refreshment, while he read again the correspondence relating to the two churches in the village of Ayot St Lawrence and the actions of the Baronet. He refused the offer of an evening meal as he was to dine at the manor, to which the landlord raised an eyebrow but wisely said nothing other than that the maid would be sure to clean Corby's shoes for him and brush down his black clerical jacket before the appointed hour.

Rachel Lyde instructed the butler to inform Sir Lionel's manservant to tell her husband that the Secretary had arrived and was coming to dine. In this way, she did not need to see her husband face to face until she was dressed for the evening and their guest had arrived. By the time she had descended from her apartments, the butler had shown Corby into the dining room where he was sitting, somewhat to his surprise, alone. Corby rose to his feet from his place at the long mahogany dining table when she entered.

She bid the Secretary take his seat. The room was bright from candles lit in a great crystal chandelier that hung in the middle of the room from the ceiling above the table, its reflection echoed again and again in the large gilt-edged mirrors on the walls, so that there were scores of chandeliers in the elegant room. Two great candelabra, with white candle wax leaking down their sides, held court on the table among the fine porcelain dishes that the servants were now depositing with care on the damask linen cloth. The butler stepped forward and poured three glasses of wine into crystal glasses; one for Corby, one for Rachel Lyde, and one for Corby's missing host, Rachel's missing husband.

"Your rooms at the Three Horseshoes are comfortable?" Rachel questioned.

"Tolerably fine, thank you, Lady Rachel," he replied.

A servant served her mistress and the guest Corby a dish of soup and ladled a portion too for the missing host.

Rachel Lyde took her soup in silence. Corby followed suit. He found her face inscrutable. She was attractive, for a lady of her age. Her fine skin feathered around the eyes, around the corners of her lips, her neck, her chest to the point where her flesh disappeared under the mousse of indistinguishable fabric froth fixed between her breasts. Her dress of teal blue, a thing of beauty and expense, was fine silk. It was embroidered with gold maple leaves; each tiny stitch glinted in the candlelight.

The soup consumed, the servants set an assortment of meat delicacies on dishes before the guest, the lady of the manor, and her missing husband.

"So Mr Corby, now that you have seen my husband's new church, may I ask you what you think of it?"

"It is…" he was lost for words to describe a building which was so much against his taste and inclination, "..modern," he finally chose.

"My husband is very proud of it," she said impassively. "He thinks that building a church will make God pleased with him and forget what he has done."

"That is no more than many church builders," Corby replied, thinking of the many churches and cathedrals across the land, across Europe, that had been funded similarly.

"Maybe so," she acquiesced, "but I would rather not be interred in a project that is for his vanity."

She finished her wine and the butler stepped forward to refill her glass. Corby noticed how her pale cheeks were now flushed rose pink.

"The Bishop will not allow the destruction of the old church, you do understand?" Corby said.

"Yet the new is built. He will not allow it to be torn down." Rachel replied evenly, as if she were an observer and not implicated in the dispute between her husband and her Bishop.

"Then your village will have two churches."

"Will the Bishop have the old church restored?"

"That, I should say, is unlikely Lady Rachel."

"What is the use of a half-ruined Church?" she asked with the curiosity of an outsider.

"A half-ruined church will serve as a useful reminder as to who owns the land."

Rachel finished the morsels that were left on her plate

"Perhaps my husband should have said 'please,'" she murmured.

The maid-servant served their third course. The first and second both still awaiting the arrival of the Baronet at his place, each dish now equally cold.

The savoury courses finished, Rachel Lyde stood up saying she would retire to her apartments where her maid would serve her a plate of sweetmeats, but Corby was welcome to stay and wait for the Baronet. She left the elegant dining room, as classical in its décor as the interior of the new Greek-style church, and swept gracefully out of the room leaving a fragrance of rose petals in her wake.

Corby accepted another glass of wine from the butler and waited. A rude, antisocial host, or an eccentric wife? He turned the situation over coolly in his head. He was on the point of bidding good evening to the silent butler, who still stood guard over the table, when the dining room doors were opened impatiently and Sir Lionel blustered in.

"Good God, you're still here? I thought you'd have realised I didn't want to see you," he addressed his guest abrasively.

Corby was momentarily taken aback, but composed himself in haste. He, the Bishop's Secretary, was not going to be bullied or browbeaten by the Baronet.

"Sir Lionel, thank you for your hospitality," he smiled ironically.

"Umph," came the courteous reply. "At least I didn't have to dine with her. You had that pleasure."

Sir Lionel took his place at the table and started to eat his meal seeming to be mindless of which foodstuff came from which course.

"You're going to tell me that I can't have my church aren't you?" the Baronet challenged Corby.

"The Bishop has no jurisdiction over how you choose to build on your own land, but he will not permit you to take down what is built on his," Corby replied.

"Umph," Sir Lionel responded eloquently. "And if I assist the elements in the weathering of the old church?"

"The weather the Almighty sends down upon His church is one thing, wilful desecration of it is another."

"And what can the Almighty do about 'wilful desecration'."

"He can speak to us through the Church courts and the Law courts."

At this, Corby saw that it was a judicious moment to leave the company of his host and he departed, knowing that his message from the Bishop had been understood; knowing that the new Palladian Church would stand in the field across from the manor; knowing that the Old Church would stand a ruin, weathered by the sun, the wind, the rain, but that no human hand would violate it further. Which of the two powerful men had won – the Baronet or the Bishop? Why, they both had of course.

8.
VODKA AND LEAD

His father had turned the heating off and now the cooling pipes, which ran like train tracks around the base of the walls, were click-clacking in strange conversations with each other. At least Chris, who was sitting on the floor, could now lean back without flinching from the burning heat of the metal. But on the other hand, it was that same heat that had kept the chill at bay, a chill that was now growing, thickening click by click. He pushed his feet further down into his sleeping bag and pulled it higher up his body to his armpits.

"Alright Chris?" his Dad asked.

Chris nodded and picked up his phone from the floor beside him to check if Daisy, his girlfriend, had answered his message yet. Nothing. He reread his two previous messages to her. He knew she must have read them and was ignoring him.

It was gloomy in the church. They'd decided not to put all the lights on to save on the electricity, just as they were saving on the heating, so only one strip above where they had made their camp was lit. Shadows crowded in on them from the unlit corners of the church. The alcoves behind the altar were hollow blanks in the eye sockets of a skull.

The light in the kitchenette and tiny lavatory, adjacent to the front door, spilt yellow into the gloom. Chris heard the toilet flush and the tap run in the handbasin.

Those who had stayed there the previous night had pushed the benches to one side and had placed some of the chairs in a square to make a room within a room. There were no pews. There had never been any pews, or so Chris's Dad, Peter, said. It meant that the church could be used as a village hall for art shows, concerts, parties, as well for services. Not that there were many services here these days, only at times of the great feasts – Easter, Harvest, Christmas.

Steve, his Dad's friend and village drinking partner at 'The Brocket Arms', turned off the kitchenette light, plunging the far end of the church into darkness, and made his way back to his sleeping place on the church floorboards. His steps echoed in the dark cavern. He worked off his shoes with his heels and his toes rather than undoing the laces. Then he wriggled into his sleeping bag.

"Alright Chris?" he asked.

Chris nodded and looked back down at his phone. Still no message. He started to compose another. How many times did he have to say he was sorry?

His Dad was reading on his Kindle, cosy in his sleeping bag, a navy fleece and beige gilet keeping his body warm, an orange beanie over his thinning grey hair, and fingerless gloves doing an insufficient job on his hands.

"God it's cold," Steve said to Peter.

"Put your gloves on," Peter advised fluttering his fingers at his friend, showing off his own.

"Didn't bring them."

"That was foolish. Nigel said they froze last night."

"He didn't tell me."

Steve put his coat on. He tucked his sleeping bag under the zip and pulled the hood over his head.

"I've got something to warm us up," Peter said after watching Steve take on the appearance of a feather-down stuffed mummy. He reached into his bag and pulled out a bottle of vodka and three small glasses.

"Ah that's my man," Steve admired, wondering why he hadn't thought to bring any himself.

Peter poured two full shots into two glasses and passed one to his friend.

"Chris, d'you want some?"

Chris looked up from his phone and nodded. His Dad poured him a double shot and handed him the glass.

"Thanks," Chris said.

"So you can talk," his Dad teased.

Chris answered with a sarcastic smirk – very funny Dad – spoken by his curled top lip. He sipped the thick cold liquid and felt it tingle-burn his lips, then his tongue, then his throat. He tipped back his head and swallowed the remainder in one gulp. He licked his lips as if a connoisseur and held out his glass to his father for a refill.

"'Struth! Is that what they teach you at uni?" Steve asked, before doing the same and holding out his glass for more vodka.

Peter drank his double shot and then refilled all three glasses.

"I bet Nigel didn't do this last night did he?" Steve commented more than asked.

"No way, he was on the rota with the vicar's husband."

"Bad luck. I can't see the vicar's husband with vodka, can you?"

"Nor beer."

"Nor wine."

Steve and Peter chuckled at the image of the vicar's husband, drunk, with Nigel Blackmore in the church in the middle of the night, but Chris kept his eyes studiously on his phone as he typed another message to Daisy using only his righthand thumb against the keypad as he was holding his second double shot of vodka in his left. Maybe he would not say sorry again. After all, it happened. He couldn't make it un-happen. He'd said sorry to her before his Mum picked him up from his halls of residence yesterday to bring him and his boxes home for the holidays. He'd sent messages on all the different platforms he knew she used. Maybe he'd play it cool now, stop saying sorry, move on and behave as if nothing had happened.

"Good of Nigel to do it, though, he's got a bad hip hasn't he?" Steve continued. "It can't have been much fun sleeping on the floor."

"Yeah." Peter agreed. "But he's not the only one, Malcolm Barnes slept over on Saturday."

"No way!" Steve exclaimed, "He's at least 80."

"More like on the way to 90," Peter corrected.

"He wouldn't have been much use if the thieves came back though. Does he know how to use a mobile?"

"I doubt it, but Colin Davies, the guy who moved in a few months ago to the Pearson's old house, went on the rota with him, and he must be only about 30."

The vodka was beginning to warm Chris's neck and chest, running its way through his veins to his fingers. He pressed too many v's and too many k's in his message to Daisy.

"How many people are helping?" Chris asked abandoning his phone, letting it drop limply down on the floorboards next to him.

"At least 20."

Twenty village men, all taking turns on a rota to sleep in the church. Twenty village men, angry that thieves had stolen the lead from the roof of their church. Lead, stolen from their community. Lead, which protected the fabric of their church, kept out the rain. It didn't matter if they didn't go into the building that regularly, it was their church, their village church. Twenty village men, any one of whom would raise the alarm, call the police, shout out and make the scum flee before they could steal any more of the black treasure and worsen the damage; each man helping out when it mattered before the security cameras could be installed.

Chris sipped his second double shot more slowly. This was a strange experience he thought, looking up at the painted white wooden ceiling of squares and circles, the white panels of Greek columns which bedecked the walls, his Dad and his Dad's best friend knocking back shots beside him, the chessboard of black and white tiles which formed a cross through the aisle of the church floor in front of him where the white tiles were now floating several inches in the air above their black partners.

"You know they say Sir Lionel Lyde, who used to own all the land round here back in the eighteenth century, visits here at night time," Steve slurred.

"I'd say 'welcome Sir Lionel' and offer him something to drink," Chris's Dad replied in a mock toast.

"Why d'you think he visits?" Chris joined in, as he watched the white tiles floating in the air.

"He built this place, didn't he? If you're going to haunt anywhere, it might as well be your own church, that you had built at great expense."

That was a good enough reason Chris thought.

"What d'yer think he'd look like?" Steve asked.

"He'd be silver-grey," said Peter.

"And he'd walk a foot off the ground," Chris added, his imagination inspired by the vodka fuelled floating tiles.

"He'd be an icy shiver tracing his finger along your arms and around your neck," Peter continued.

"Blimey you do get poetic when you drink," his friend praised.

Peter gave Steve a lopsided smile of gratitude.

Chris's phone vibrated on the floor beside him – a message. He grabbed it quickly, and in his clumsy haste, it jumped out of his hand, forcing him to scramble for it even more clumsily.

"Careful mate," Steve advised, not looking himself any more able to reach for a phone, since he too had downed two double shots and was contemplating another.

Chris ignored him. He screwed up his eyes to read the message in the gloom and then raised his eyebrows high into his forehead in an attempt to keep the words on the small phone screen in one place so he could read them. It was from Caitlin. Fuck! She didn't know the trouble she'd caused him. But maybe not 'fuck,' at least Caitlin appeared to be speaking to him.

"Woman trouble," Peter mouthed to his friend in what came out as a loud stage whisper.

"Ahh," Steve nodded. Woman trouble. He had enough of that himself with Alex his ex-wife constantly whinging and Mona his on-off girlfriend mostly off it seemed.

"Sir Lionel had woman trouble didn't he?"

"Yeah, his wife hated him."

"Perhaps the feeling was mutual," Steve said, thinking of Alex.

The temperature was dropping further and now raindrops pattered on the plain glass windows high above their heads. After a few moments, it grew heavier. The rain threw pebbles on the roof and a gust of wind tugged at the front door making it creak and groan.

"Not a night for thieves," Peter commented, holding out the vodka bottle towards Steve to see if he wanted anymore. Steve thought maybe he should refuse, but as the thieves plainly weren't going to bother them, more vodka didn't seem a problem.

Chris's phone vibrated. Caitlin again. He liked Caitlin, she was always ready to laugh and was just as hopeless as he was at getting to lectures on time. She was pretty too. When she kissed him as they had left the bar together on Friday night she pushed her tongue into his mouth and searched him, probed him. She had her eyes open as she kissed him, and he read in their blackness, 'imagine what I could do with my hands, how I would touch, how I would probe.'

Suddenly, the growling wind tore at the door, gripping it with its nails and wrenching it open with a clatter that made the three men jump. A cold blast of air entered the church accompanied by the angry patter of rain, fierce drops bouncing off the portico, crashing on the stone steps. An icy shiver traced its fingers along their arms and around their necks. It pressed against their collarbones and pushed frozen hands onto their chests, squeezing their breath. Chris's shot glass dropped from his hand. It fell hard against the floor and shattered, sending sparkling crystals flying. Peter's followed. Then Steve's.

"What's that?" Steve gasped, eyes bulging.

"Sir Lionel Lyde?" Peter coughed, pushing fearfully against the coldness clutching at his chest.

The open church door creaked on its hinges and out in the darkness beyond, there came scratching on the stone steps, heavy breathing, yellow eyes in the blackness.

Chris dived deep into his sleeping bag, attempting to pull the mouth over his head to hide in a primitive attempt to keep himself safe.

The scratching came closer. It was bounding through the door and leaping at Chris in his sleeping bag, a tongue was searching for him. Not Caitlin's he thought in horror, a wet, rough, vigorous, saliva slipping tongue.

"Kaiser, that's enough," a woman's voice commanded. A strong hand pulled Kaiser off Chris.

"Thought you'd be needing us," his mother smiled down at him when Chris opened his eyes. Kaiser had turned his watery attention to Peter.

"You've got yourselves in a bit of a mess haven't you?" Sharon continued, noting the frosting of shot glasses on the floor and overturned vodka bottle.

"What happened here? Or need I ask?"

"Sir Lionel Lyde," Steve replied apologetically and incomprehensively.

"I see," Sharon said. But she didn't.

"You shouldn't have come," Peter chastised, feeling he ought to have the upper hand over his wife somehow. "The weather's vile."

"So you'll refuse the hot chocolate and marshmallows I've brought you for your boys' camping night?"

None of the men looked as if they would refuse.

In an instant, she had found the dustpan and brush in the cupboard, cleared up the shattered glass from the floor, and distributed fresh glasses of water from the kitchenette tap to counteract the vodka. Finally, she poured four mugs of steaming syrupy, creamy chocolate from her flask. She wrapped her legs in the picnic blanket she had bought and snuggled up to her husband for warmth.

"Now what's this about Sir Lionel?" she asked.

But Chris couldn't answer, his phone had vibrated again; a message from Daisy. Sharon saw her son pull an anguished face as he read.

"Woman trouble," Peter mouthed to her.

"Alright Chris?" she asked kindly.

"Daisy's dumped me," he replied, almost inaudibly.

"Never mind mate," Steve consoled holding out the vodka bottle where some of the clear liquid still lingered at the bottom, clinging like syrup to the glass. "Have another shot."

Chris thought for a moment about the additional morning headache more vodka would bring. Caitlin still liked him. That was comforting.

"Thanks, but I'd rather have hot chocolate."

9.
THE ART SHOW AT AYOT

Lisa bent her head closer to the wall, so she could study the tiny details in the small watercolour painting that hung in her sister-in-law's hall. She had not seen it before. Sophie had acquired it since her last visit. The little painting was so like the ones Lisa had at home in Boston, but it was a different view. Not face on to the white colonnades, buttercup-filled field in the foreground, but at a slight slant, beige-fleeced sheep grazing at the side. It was strange, she thought, how she could know so well a place she had visited so few times. She recognised the style of the painter, of course, as well as the familiar initials in the right-hand corner: C.W. Colin Williams.

Colin had been surprised to receive the hand-written notecard with an unusual pastel sketch of the Palladian Church. Most correspondence these days was electronic. A lady from the States, who had a small collection of his work, was intending to visit this year's art show in the church at Ayot St Lawrence. She would be attending the preview on the Friday evening. She noticed he was exhibiting and wanted to know if he would be there in person? She hoped so.

He wondered briefly if she had drawn the church herself, it wasn't signed. The familiar image conjured by this unknown artist was at once haunting and graceful. Mauves and greys of the palette prevented the actual greens of the chosen season from entering the scene. Naïve, amateur in its rendering, the pastel smudges created a fragility that was forever lost to him the expert – a smoke shape that his honed talent could never again grasp. He held the notecard picture out before him, letting light and shade play over the pastel feeling both intrigued and flattered.

Yes, he would be at the preview and would make a point of looking out for her. Although, as the art show was a notable local event with a considerable fundraising element for the conservation of an iconic Hertfordshire landmark, the evening was likely to be busy. He enclosed a preview invitation from his allocation in case she had not been able to procure one from elsewhere.

A warm June day had melted into a heaven-sent summer evening. The normally tranquil church was a hive of activity. Having previewed and purchased, guests sipped Prosecco on the steps. Under the portico, a jazz band performed, framed by a statuesque arrangement of lilies and roses. The perfumed music of summer drifted lazily over the buzz of transaction and evening leisure.

"Are you interested in any particular artist?" a well-groomed volunteer welcomed the two floral dressed ladies at the marquee entrance.

"No, just browsing," Lisa lied.

"Oh, you come from America!"

Lisa allowed the faintest of polite smiles to play on her lips in response and craned her neck to glimpse the art on display beyond. Everyone has history and she did not want hers to be exhibited for all to see on the steps of the church.

"My sister-in-law is visiting from Boston, but I'm local," Sophie replied apologetically on Lisa's behalf. The culprit had already moved on and was honouring a glorious acrylic peacock, the painted welcome to the annual event.

"Lisa," Sophie said in a low voice, "she was just trying to be pleasant."

"I have no desire to open up my life to strangers," came the terse response.

Sophie sighed, she knew Lisa was lonely but sometimes she could just be so – so brittle.

The peacock's feathers gleamed in the sunlight, a spectacle of blues, greens, and purples in a regal frame of gold. His piercing black eyes demanding "are you as beautiful as me?" The red sticker of purchase in the corner evidence that he was admired as much as he commanded and would forevermore adorn a wall and be eternally worshipped.

Alongside the peacock hung three fruit ready to eat; an orange, a lemon, and a pineapple their skins smooth and scratchy. Modern-day Dutch masterpieces, standing bright in sombre black darkness, as a lone candle lights the world. Framed modestly but exquisitely in dark wood. Beauty in simplicity. Extraordinary in the ordinary.

Next, the Palladian Church – a Greek temple in a Hertfordshire field – a perfect English oxymoron presented in acrylic, watercolour, and pastel from a distance, close up, looking down, looking up, in whole and in part. The same subject portrayed, but each piece unique, as a day is never the same, as you yourself are never the same each time you gaze, in a different mood, always older than the moment before; as looking for the second, third, fourth time is never the same as seeing for the first. The Palladian Church, constant and ageless, bit by bit worn down by the weather and visitors but never the same, except for CW in the right-hand corner. Initials now joined by a splattering of red stickers on the frames as if Jackson Pollock had scarletised his brush and flicked the tips of his fingers to scatter blood-specs randomly across the display to settle in an unexpected artistic form.

Standing in St Lawrence's eighteenth-century interior, Lisa gazed at the montage of its exterior, which hung before her in multifarious beautiful perspectives like cut glass crystal. She was in the building's heart. The preview crowds surrounded her with their purchase chats, admiration, and criticism, seemingly unaware of where they were and what they were looking at. But she, Lisa, was smiling at the art in the building's heart.

"Such a shame so many have sold," Sophie commented, approaching the display panel. She, like her sister-in-law, was a fan of Colin Williams' work. "Do you like any of the rest?"

Together the friend relatives examined the crystal perspectives of the Palladian church under its changing skies.

Colin cast his eyes around the exhibition. He wondered if she would, indeed, come this evening. Or perhaps she was already here? He had no idea how old she might be or even what ethnicity. Did an American woman dress differently from an English woman? She had the advantage of being able to recognise him, as an artist of modest reputation, he knew his portrait photo could be found on the internet. The irony of the artist viewing the audience as carefully as the audience viewed the artist's work did not escape him.

"How is it going this evening Colin?" Ralph, a tall grey-bearded fellow painter asked. Colin glanced at the boards where his friend's work was displayed and, noting that red stickers were absent, replied tactfully,

"Okay, but it's bound to slow down."

"Not yet," Ralph chuckled with no hint of jealousy. "Seems like you're in line to sell another."

The two men looked over to the boards where Colin's paintings hung and observed a pair of friends in summer floral dresses who were engrossed in an enthusiastic discussion of the art.

"Ladies," Colin greeted Sophie and Lisa warmly, "may I be of assistance?"

Momentarily Lisa was shocked by the colour incarnation of the internet black and white portrait she had seen. He was paler and warmer in the flesh. There he stood before her, the honey beige of his linen trousers complimenting the sandy grey-blonde of his hair, his aqua eyes the exact light blue shade of his shirt. Flushed with embarrassment, she looked away to examine the nearest watercolour.

The slightly taller of the two ladies replied,

"Thank you, are you Colin Williams?"

"Yes, that's me."

"My sister-in-law is looking for an unusual view of the church to add to her collection," Sophie took control, embarking upon the green shoots of a transaction.

The slightly smaller copper-haired lady turned self-consciously from the watercolour to the man,

"Mr Williams, I wrote to you..."

"Lisa from Boston!" Colin beamed. "Tell me, was it you who drew the picture on your card?"

Sophie's negotiation came to a dead halt with this unexpected exchange. Her fiercely private relation friend, writing to this handsome artist and sending him a drawing she had done herself! Looking from one face to the other, she refrained from entering their first conversation.

"Yes, it was. It's not so good, I know." Lisa blushed, maybe sending her pastel hadn't been such a great idea after all.

"I really liked it," the honesty in his blue eyes was as clear as the hue. "In fact, your colours inspired me...."

He reached around to the back of the display boards to bring out a view of the Palladian church in a modern grey frame. It was the same view that Lisa had chosen and in identical colours but now it was silky dusk, the magical moment when daytime slips into night, the soft seconds where the end of the day turns into the new of the night.

Un-noticed by the artists deep in conversation, Sophie moved quietly back to the entrance with a smile, to admire the peacock and to enjoy the summer jazz with a glass of prosecco.

10.
PYGMALION

It was the moment she most enjoyed in all of her shows, the shiver of anticipation as the audience quietened, settling themselves into their seats, turning their attention to the business of being entertained. The sick feeling of 'will they like it?' 'will they understand?' 'will everything be okay?' balanced on a tightrope with the certainty that the play is well-rehearsed, the cast well-chosen, the subtexts clear enough to be noticed but not lit up in neon lights. If tonight were one of her musical productions, then there would be an orchestra tuning up in the pit, producing a cacophony of jumbled notes that would reach a pitch of excitement and gently subside into silence – the signal that the show is ready to begin.

She looked around the garden at her audience seated on picnic chairs scattered across the lawn; through the centre, around the edges, almost in the bushes and the flowerbeds. Half an hour ago there had been the sound of chatting, eating, and drinking. Now there was stillness. Half an hour ago the audience had been hung like a bunch of grapes in small groups across the lawn. Now they were all faced towards the stage, the terrace at the back of the house, and each person had manoeuvred themselves into a position for the best view. Where had they all come from she wondered? Were they locals, with homes in Ayot St Lawrence? Had some travelled far? She knew that the play had been advertised widely by the National Trust, who owned Shaw's

Corner, there had been posters, social media posts, magazine and newspaper advertisements. How many had seen a production in these fabulous grounds before and for whom was this their first time – their first experience of the magic?

It had been a perfect July evening. So often with outdoors productions, the weather was against you, Juliet mused. There could be rain, or it could be off-puttingly cold. The worst, almost, was the wind which snatched the actors' words away from their mouths and raced with their syllables far from the ears of the audience. Tonight there was not one breath of air. Her actors could whisper their lines and their words would bounce off the arts and crafts red brickwork of the house behind them and onto the lawn. A pin could drop and it would be heard.

There was no curtain, as this was not a theatre. The terrace stage was already set with a table, a chair and a very small sofa – Higgins' house. The Covent Garden scenes would take place further forward on the grass, almost on the laps of the front row of the audience. This meant that there was minimal set change for the small troupe to cope with. But it also marked a different space, the place where Eliza was found, the place where she was her natural original self, before the men tried to change her. The stage is the space where she becomes different, where they turn her into what she is not, it is a man-made place where men have laid patio stone over the natural ground.

Her cast members were behind the screens placed at the end of the terrace to act as wings and which hid from the audience the props table, their bottles of water, the rail with the costumes for changes required later in the play and, of course, their scripts, ready to act as prompts for words and stage directions. Juliet had been in the wings many, many times herself. She knew what would be going through each actor's head as they waited for the show to begin. Sitting in her place at the back, surrounded by her audience and George Bernard Shaw's shrubs, she could feel what each one of her cast was feeling. Seema, her beautiful Eliza, would be a spring about to uncoil at the edge of the screen, holding her basket of flowers, ready to leap onto the stage like a fresh morning sunrise. Connor, her reliable Colonel Pickering, would be alongside her, pulling her back in so that she wouldn't go beyond the boundary of the screen and be seen by the audience before the play started. A father of two teenage girls himself and an experienced stagehand, he had been a dream to work with, giving Seema balance and grounding. Anthony, her eccentric gay Higgins, would be fussing in front of his bathroom travel mirror, which he always kept in the wings to check his hair, his teeth, and smile before each entrance and after each exit. Harry, her young Freddy, would be nonchalantly chewing gum until the very last minute, whereupon he would take it out of his mouth and wrap it up for later use. Each actor would be anxious and excited in their own way.

It was a perfect night for a play. Juliet felt that never before had a play and place and a night been so right. She had been surprised when she had received an email from Stuart at Playhouse Touring Productions six months ago. She'd worked with Stuart in the past, but not since the flop of *Richard III*. It had all been rather embarrassing, and not her fault in the slightest, they all acknowledged that now. The play had been well directed by her and Stuart had produced it beautifully, the cast had done as valiantly as could be expected under the circumstances, it was just that the audience hadn't been ready for the interpretation. It had left a bad taste in the mouth. The flop had not damaged Stuart's business, after all, you win some, you lose some, but somehow they had both felt embarrassed, like friends who had crossed the boundary between friendship and lovers, only to find it had been a mistake and the new intimacy turned the friendship sour with unwanted, regretted physical knowledge of each other. They had found excuses not to bump into each other, hadn't proposed any projects like they once had. Until Stuart asked her to direct *Pygmalion* for him at Shaw's Corner.

Pygmalion, the iconic story of Eliza Doolittle, written by George Bernard Shaw, to be performed outside in the great writer's own garden. How could she say no?

She had no intention of serving up the audience anything other than what they expected this time. There was to be no change of period, no nudity, just pure and simply the story of Higgins changing Eliza from flower girl to lady, leaving her with nowhere to fit in. The power would be where it always had been – in the play itself – delivered by an outstanding cast.

Juliet had known she wanted Seema for Eliza from the moment Seema had walked through the door into the church hall Stuart had hired for audition day. Seema was tall and willowy. She had luxurious long dark hair, thick and shiny, which floated over her shoulders and down her back. She wore a tight white crop top and low cut denim jeans with fashionably cut holes at the knees. At the space where her jeans did not meet her top, a diamante drop hung in her belly button, from a gold stud fixed in her toned golden-wheat skin. The diamante drop caught the light as Seema moved, glimmering and beckoning Juliet to touch it, to touch Seema's perfect flat stomach.

"Hi, I'm Seema," she had announced without fear, dazzling Juliet with her bright black eyes.

As Seema had read the part, Juliet could not take her eyes off her. Everything about the young woman was perfect. She was the right age, scarcely more than 20, she had divinely shaped eyebrows, soft luscious red lips, a way of moving that was one moment childish and inexperienced, a girl who didn't know quite what a woman she was, but the next moment a young woman who pulsed with potential. Seema, Juliet knew, would captivate and charm the audience with her interpretation of Eliza.

Rob, the stage manager, poked his head around the edge of the screen furthest from the edge of the stage. He scanned for Juliet in the audience and their eyes locked. All was ready backstage, all was ready in the house. Silently, Juliet raised a thumbs up. Rob nodded and his head disappeared back behind the screen. Her cast spilt onto the stage. Her play had begun.

Higgins strutted arrogantly around the stage, confident in the rightness of manipulation; Pickering caught in the desire to see the experiment through and the effect it was having on Eliza; inept and unexciting Freddy – Eliza's obvious way out; and Eliza Doolittle – beautiful, radiant Seema.

Seema hadn't found the part easy, for all her bravado at the audition. She slipped naturally into the skin of Covent Garden Eliza – the cockney accent, the lack of finesse. She conveyed the desire to change and to please Higgins, but somehow she could not quite reach the place of the confident Princess who hides her real self from the world.

Juliet knew she had been right to cast Seema but worried about how to help Seema break through. She followed Seema's movements constantly in rehearsal, she went over in her head the way Seema had delivered her lines. Seema. The name sounded like a sigh of desire, like an ebb and a flow, pushing away with the 'see' and drawing back in with 'ma'. Seema's hair smelt of lemons. It surprised Juliet who expected the thick dark tresses to be pure musk. The citrus scent caught her by surprise, like tasting traditional Victorian fruitcake which you expect to be dark and fruity rich but is, when you bite into it, lemon zest fresh.

"The trouble is," Stuart had said over coffee, just two weeks ago, when the tickets were all sold out and the play was at full costume runs and Seema still seemed unable to find the princess in her character. "The trouble is," he repeated, "the trouble is, Juliet, you fancy her."

There! He'd said it now. After the *Richard III* debacle, he'd found it impossible to talk openly with Juliet, but now at last he'd said what he'd noticed since the audition.

"That's not true," Juliet protested, putting her coffee down on the table firmly and crossing her legs and her arms to allow no penetration, give away no secrets. She raised her right hand to her mouth and chewed her nail nervously.

"Really?" Stuart raised his eyes. "Not my type, but she is stunning."

"Shut up, Stuart," Juliet snapped. "You're completely wrong."

Of course he was wrong. There was no way she fancied Seema. Seema was too young, way too young for her. She loved the flesh, the curves, the intoxication of a woman like Seema but that was what she wanted a woman; not a girl. A woman who knew how to satisfy her, how to touch her in those intimate unknown places, who knew without being asked, without being shown. She was lonely since Bea had left her. She had flung herself into her work, but she pined for the relaxed contentment of wrapping her limbs around another woman, pressing her face into soft breasts, and holding another woman close to her own.

Juliet shifted her weight uneasily on her chair. Stuart was still looking at her with his eyebrows raised, as if he had read every word she had just thought, as if she had delivered them as a monologue in the café.

"Look Juliet, I don't mind what you do in the future, really I don't, just don't do anything now. Don't make any kind of move on her until after the show."

Since Stuart had spoken Juliet hadn't been able to stop thinking about Seema openly in her thoughts, rather than secretly, hiding from her subconscious. Now the genie was out of her bottle, she scoured Seema's intonation in their conversations, in her movements, to try to read what Seema felt about her. Was a look from those dancing dark eyes an invitation or was it an actress' enjoyment in playing a part? Juliet made sure that Connor was constantly present as an oblivious chaperone.

The final dress rehearsal arrived, the last run through and the first and only rehearsal at Shaw's Corner to a lawn empty of picnic chairs and watchers. Seema was still perfect, until the transition. Juliet bit her nails anxiously as she waited for the run to begin. She knew it was the only thing wrong with the show, the only aspect that the critics would come down upon and Seema didn't deserve it. It was her fault as the director that Seema had not dived far enough into the depths. She looked beautiful though as the princess, the white satin dress encasing her breasts and hips in silky elegance, highlighting her soft wheat skin and luscious ebony locks, quickly swept up and fixed with a comb to allow for the swift costume change. Stuart had arrived at the rehearsal earlier with the period jewellery set he had borrowed for her: a stunning diamante necklace with matching drop earrings.

When Seema stepped onto the stage in the open air, on George Bernard Shaw's terrace, the transformation was complete. The final touch to the costume and the mystery of being Eliza in George Bernard Shaw's garden, where he that great writer had imagined and created Eliza, wove its magic. Seema gave of herself as much in the hidden-false Princess Eliza as she did in the authentic cockney. Juliet's eyes welled with sweet tears of relief.

Now, this evening, Seema held her audience, each one, in the palm of her hand. Each and every spectator fell in love with her that night. As the minutes passed, the evening warmth stayed balmy, the daylight dimmed and tiny pricks of starlight began to appear in the cobalt blue sky. The terrace, lit only with daylight in the first act, was now flooded with bright stage light.

The applause echoed around the garden. It bounced off the walls of Shaw's Corner. Dozens of audience members were on their feet, clapping enthusiastically.

"Bravo! Bravo!"

Bravo indeed.

The performers took their bows and then Colonel Pickering, Connor, beckoned to Juliet to come on to the stage with Stuart for acknowledgement. She didn't want to. She would have preferred to have stayed on the lawn, watching her actors, watching her audience. But Stuart, never one to be shy of praise, pulled her to her feet and pushed her onto the stage. Seema grabbed Juliet by the hand and led her to stand next to her in the lamplight. Momentarily, Juliet was bewildered, dazzled by the mobile stage lights in her eyes, the sound of the applause, and the cheers; overwhelmed by the pulse of electricity travelling up her arm from her palm to her neck, from the insistent squeeze of Seema's fingers held tightly in her own.

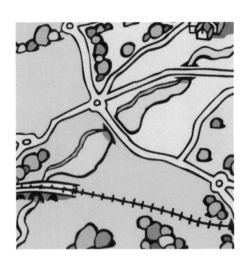

PART 2:
FIELD, LANE, AND RIVER

11.
PATHS OF PESTILENCE

Thomas Ditton rode his horse at a trot along the lane from St Albans to Wheathamsptead and then home to Codicote. He urged the old mare to a pace that the beast resented. Why hurry, she thought to herself when they did not usually hurry home from the market? Why hurry, when spring was here and juicy fresh grass along the wayside was welcome refreshment after the hay of winter? Why hurry, when there had already been the press of the morning, the insistency of every week's journey to the market at St Albans?

Every day of the year, Thomas rose with the sun in the summer or the pitch-dark stillness in winter. In those long night months, he would shrink from leaving the covers of his bed, the warmth of his wife. He would force his feet to the wooden floor of his bedchamber and, shivering, pull his knitted hose over his legs and heave on his tall leather boots. His wife Joan, feeling the coldness of the empty space in the bed beside her, would then waken herself and would now rise quickly to dress in her hose and tunic, wrapping herself in a shawl to keep out the morning chill, and make her way to the kitchen to light the fire.

If it were market day at St Albans, as it had been this morning, Joan would prepare his luncheon, stowing it safely in a pouch for him to eat later in the day if trade permitted. Then together, husband and wife would load the rolls of cloth stored in their house, into the back of their cart. They had performed this task so often over the years that they were efficient in their movements, not needing to comment one to the other, as they took hold of either end of each bolt of fabric and laid it in the cart. The horse would stamp her feet in the stable and whinny, anxious to depart once her ears had heard the herald of the day's routine. All had happened this morning as it happened every market day that Thomas Ditton, Codicote cloth merchant, and his horse could remember.

It was nine miles ride to St Albans. The market, close to the Benedictine Abbey, provided the most lucrative trade of his week. Joan sold cloth from the hatch at the front of their house, which gave onto the village high street, every day except for the village market day when Thomas set up his stall, and for the Sabbath, the day of rest. This brought in a healthy amount of coins to their household coffers, but the real trade was in the town, and nine miles there and nine miles back was not too high a price to pay for it.

What was more, Thomas enjoyed market days. He enjoyed driving his horse and cart along the lanes which he had travelled every market day since a boy. His keen eyes noticed the changes that each week brought. Now, at the end of April, later than the other trees, the oak was permitting its fresh yellow-green leaves to curl out from the buds that had pimpled the twigs and branches since the autumn. In no more than a fortnight the acorn blossom would be flowering, unobserved by all but him. By Whitsuntide, the spring foliage would be darkening to summer rich green, its adult hue, which it would retain until the nights of autumn grew longer, and the sun paler, turning those same leaves brown. In November, when the chill winds blew, the elderly oak leaves would strain to cling to the boughs and to the twigs, long after the leaves of the Hawthorne, the Ash, and the Beech had given up hope of clinging on to their home and had tumbled dead to the ground. The last oak leaves of the year would remain fast, until the feast of the Christ Child, when they would silently relinquish their grasp and flutter to the earth below. Thomas saw it all.

Each market day he would drive the cart into the centre of the town, where he would stable his horse for the day at his preferred inn for a small expense; an expense which included the assistance of the innkeeper's boy to unload the bolts of fabric onto Thomas' stall. The first visitors of the morning to his stall would be the housewives seeking cloth for all manner of garments and domestic necessity; from tunics to sheets, from cloth for the welcome of new babes to lengths for the shrouds of the departed. Next to arrive would be the pilgrims, bringing their spiritual devotion to the shrine of Alban the saint. The pilgrims gathered here from all over the country, Thomas knew, from the sound of their tongues and the information they imparted. No matter. Pilgrims still have coins in their pockets and fine cloth is fine cloth, wherever it is sold. Last came the travellers, for St Albans offered the first of the coach-house stops on the journey north from London and the last on the journey south.

Thomas stabled his horse and with the assistance of the inn keeper's boy stocked his stall, piling some rolls of fabric high and spreading others out to reveal their colours, their textures, their desirability. He took up his usual position behind his wares, feet placed firmly on the ground, slightly apart, and hands behind his back. He was not to know that it was the last time he would ever stand in that place in such a way.

At the Abbey, the pinched face of brother Francis opened the gate to a small band of pilgrims seeking hospitality. He was unsure of what to do. They had been instructed by their Abbott, may the Lord bless his soul, and the Abbott before him, and the one before him, to extend hospitality to all pilgrims. To serve pilgrims, come to the shrine of the Saint, was to serve Christ Himself. But the sickness was bad. So very bad. A sickness had stolen into the Abbey at Easter, like a thief in the night. No one had foreseen it. Holy week had been holy on Palm Sunday, but by Maundy Thursday it had putrefied. Abbott Michael was sick. He had presided over High Mass and washed the feet of his flock – brothers and pilgrims – just as their Lord Jesus Christ had done; but the Abbott's face was flushed in heat, his hand shook as he humbly bathed and dried toes, soles, heels. Brother Andrew assisted him to his chamber and lay the Abbott down in his bed, covering him tenderly with a blanket. The Abbott did not rise the following day. He was not with the brothers to contemplate the breaking of Christ's body on the cross. Instead, his own body was breaking. Brother Andrew reported, worriedly and in hushed whispers, that boils the size of hen's eggs had appeared overnight on the Abbott's body at his groin and at his throat.

Brother Nathanael, from the hospice, blessed with the gift of healing, prepared tinctures of thyme and marjoram to spoon between the Abbott's cracked lips and warm poultices of bran and lavender, which he spread over Abbott

Michael's swelling, anguished body, attempting to draw the fever from his head, the poison from his flesh. He cared for the Abbott as if the man was a little child. But to no avail. Jesus Christ was brought to life on Easter day, but not Abbott Michael, who on that morn drew his last breath.

That very evening Brother Andrew took to his bed, the fever coming fast upon him. The buboes in the poor man's armpits and thighs grew almost to the size of geese eggs. His agonising death screams brought the remaining brothers to their knees in desperate pleas to the Lord for mercy. They carried on with their duties as best they could with cloth over their noses and their mouths so as not to breathe the bad air on which surely this pestilence was born. When they wrapped Brother Andrew's body in the shroud which would be his last garment, his fingers were black from the nail to the knuckle as if he had been gardening with bare hands in rich soil.

Brother Francis wondered anxiously what he should do, he pulled in his bottom lip and chewed on it as was his habit when unsure.

The pilgrim at the front of the band of four reached his hand out and placed it firmly on the door which separated the band seeking welcome and the expected welcome within. So close was his hand to the hand of the frightened brother Francis, that their fingers almost touched.

"What is this?" the man asked. "Surely the famous hospitality of the monks of the Abbey of St Alban is not being refused to us poor pilgrims?"

"Nay, good sir," Brother Francis replied meekly, deciding to open the door, deciding to extend the welcome, but not to impart the bad news.

"The brothers of the Abbey welcome you indeed."

Of the four pilgrims who entered, only two would leave.

The following day was market day, and that same pilgrim who had demanded his right of hospitality, having prayed to the saint for forgiveness and for rich blessings from which forgiveness flowed, strolled past the stalls in St Peter's Street. He passed by the fresh produce with disinterest. He approached the woodturners stall, where he spent a good length of time examining the bowls and the spoons, the trinket boxes and the toys; picking wares up, asking the woodturner questions, before placing each down and proceeding to the next stall, himself more wealthy in knowledge and the wood-turner feeling out of pocket.

The pilgrim made his way along the row of stalls until at last, he stopped in front of Thomas' fabric.

"Fine cloth good Master," he complimented Thomas.

"The best in Heorotfrodsir," Thomas exaggerated, because he felt like it.

"Maybe so," the pilgrim concurred. "How much?" he continued pointing at a neatly folded pile of grey-weave squares, several yards each in length.

"Two pennies a yard," Thomas replied.

"And this?" The pilgrim asked Thomas, reaching for a length of dark red worsted, pulling it towards him from its resting place on the stall to eye level. As he did so, a tiny dark flea crept from the folds at the wrist of his tunic and hopped onto the worsted. A tiny flea, a deadly flea, a flea that was already well-travelled from a rat to a cat, to a rat, to a man, to an Abbott, to a monk, to a pilgrim, to a bolt of dark red worsted.

"Six pennies a yard," Thomas replied.

The pilgrim winced at the cost.

"Five pennies?" the Pilgrim proposed.

"Six pennies," Thomas asserted.

The day was still young, Thomas need not budge yet on the price of his best worsted.

"I will take four yards of your grey-weave," the Pilgrim settled upon, leaving the flea safely on the red worsted on Thomas' stall.

Pestilence. The word passed from one stall-holder to the next. Pestilence. The syllables were mouthed fearfully from pilgrim to pilgrim. Pestilence? A traveller overheard. Not here, surely not here? London maybe but surely not St Albans? The Abbott dead at the Abbey. Five brothers more in their graves alongside him, a dozen more sickening and pilgrims too. The stall-holders hurried to pack away their wares and be gone, anxious to leave the town of too many people, too close together with too much foul air. If St Alban could not keep the Abbey safe from disease what chance did ordinary folk have?

Thomas loaded his bolts of fabric onto his cart, pausing to scratch at an itch under his armpit.

He fought hard for his life, struggling against the fever coursing through his body, straining against the poisons in his veins, forcing his lungs to pull in air to keep him alive. His head tossed from side to side on the pillow. He had no control over his legs and arms which thrashed and beat. He knew not that his body was emptying itself of all fluids onto the bed in which he had slept alongside his wife for more than twenty years. Throughout all, Joan held her husband, his hand or his arm. She bathed his head, tied the toad to his breast that the doctor advised. For three days and nights she scarcely slept, so tightly did she hold, so violently did she will him to be the victor in the fight. It was not to be. In the early hours of the fourth morning, Death entered their house and plucked Thomas to take him to stand before the gates of Heaven with one Abbott, ten monks, and four pilgrims. Death left Thomas there for he knew not what, and returned to Heorotfrodsir to continue the pestilent harvest.

She cried until there were no more tears to be shed. So many she cried, she could have washed the sick room, the death room, with their briny wetness alone. She cut a length of his finest red worsted for his shroud. When his body was cleansed, his hair brushed, sweet-smelling herbs tucked between his limbs, she stitched it closed herself, entombing her fine husband in his finest cloth. 'Shocking' some villagers would say, 'shameful' others would add. Was a simple, cheap cloth not good enough for a cloth merchant? they would all think silently in their heads as they watched the dead man take his last journey to the graveyard at the village church.

Thomas Ditton was laid in the ground. The very next morn the week turned a full seven days and it was market day again. His widow, Joan, rode the old horse to the town, the bolts of fabric still loaded where Thomas had left them on his ill-fated return. She travelled the lanes from Codicote to Wheathamsptead, from Wheathampstead to St Albans; nine miles there and nine miles back. She travelled these lanes to market in the winter, the spring, the summer, and the autumn all-told for more than 20 years a widow. She travelled these lanes because life goes on as winter turns to spring, because each household needs an income and because a tiny black flea had landed on red worsted and had found her husband a welcome host.

12.

THE RIVER

Golden sunshine played merrily with the cool deep waters of the willow pool. Ripples of crystal light danced over its bubbling surface as if joining in the bankside birthday party for the Queen of the river folk.

By the waterside, a long-haired beauty plucked an ancient melody from her harp accompanied by a long-limbed man on a flute. The summer notes carried on the air up and downstream, far and wide from the banks, delighting the four points of the compass.

On the grass beneath the willows, dozens of liveried servants offered shining glasses, as delicate as dragonfly wings and filled with fizzing nectar, to elegant guests. Dozens more bore silver platters of sweet delicacies, each morsel served on a rose petal plate. Beautiful ladies and handsome gentlemen smiled and flirted in the sunshine beside the river's pool.

Moving from guest to guest the Queen thanked each for their presence and their gifts, accepting the refreshment and enjoying the music as much as any. She wore a sleeveless dress of palest green, as light as chiffon, which floated down her slender form. Her blonde hair flowed around her shoulders and her breasts. For modesty, and to protect herself from the later evening chill, she wore a silver spider's web shawl into which she, with her own hand, had sewn freshwater pearls. Her subjects curtseyed and bowed, their faces radiating admiration and obedience, for she was a much-loved monarch for her gentleness and generosity.

A long grey tree trunk, felled for many a year, lay on the bank. Lemon tinted moss, so downy, so soft, had grown over the tough bark to form a velvet-covered sofa of satisfying comfort. Here perched a fairy youth looking, for all to see, anything but comfortable. Buttoned tightly into breeches and shirt which had fitted last summer, he stared mutinously at the grass beneath his feet. Arms and legs full of constrained energy, like an arrow in a taut bow ready to let fly at the sight of the hunter's prey.

"Please do try a glass of the nectar," he heard a lovely voice address him. "I am sure you are old enough now, you have grown so tall and I have heard tell of your growing good sense."

Determined mutiny raised his adolescent eyes to the speaker and in so doing the dark black irises grew wide in shock. Scrambling awkwardly to his new-size feet he managed an ungainly bow. His heart raced, pumping blood to the broadening limbs bringing the power to run like a frightened rabbit in an exposed field from the view of the hawk to the safety of the burrow. How hideous, how awful, how embarrassing to be noticed by the Queen and to be expected to find speech! Regaining his balance, he transferred his weight nervously from foot to foot, not yet having learned to hide his feelings behind stillness.

But the Queen was not a hawk in search of prey; she was a thoughtful, caring woman.

"Please Tom, do sit – my sofa is comfortable is it not? Tell me about your bow and arrows. I have heard that you practise in the fields and I can see for myself how strong you are becoming." Her mezzo tones were soothing, like the sound of the river flowing over pebbles, and no more would you expect, for the river was her birthplace and her home.

The anxious colt calmed with a few more kind words, was drawn to conversation, of sorts, and began to smile at the thought of his fine bow and his muscled arm. Pride, well deserved, straightened his spine and he held his head a little higher. Amongst all the beautiful and handsome guests Her Majesty had spoken to him – Tom! Only fifteen summers had he seen, yet she had spoken to him! Her work done, she moved gracefully away and he watched his fairy Queen approach an elderly couple enjoying the riverside concert. He saw their happy faces light up to full mid-day brightness at her arrival and he regarded this most divine of water nymphs bestow her subtle gift upon them.

How happy his lovely Queen appeared and even more so when the harp and flute gave way to fairy pipes, signalling it was time to dance. Fairy couples flew over the bank laughing and smiling in the air, on the land, across the water. The Queen danced as much as any, her green dress rippling under her waterfall shawl. So like a waterfall was the shawl that, as she danced, the pearl-encrusted spider's web fell from her shoulders into the water, where it floated for a second lazily on the pool's surface before drifting away from the party, pulled by the current in the direction of the ford which marked the magical boundary of its owner's kingdom.

In a fraction of an instant, Tom sped from his moss couch high into the air. He was a fired arrow cutting high and swooping low to the surprise of the dancers. He landed with a splash in the ford, exhilarated by action and filled with the desire to rescue the royal garment.

"No!"

"Tom!"

Voices cried out behind him.

He did not heed their warning. He reached for the shawl and almost had it in hand, but he slipped on the road surface and it escaped him, finding speed in the current as the river raced away from the ford. Tom gave purpose to his body, instructing it to rise as a bird into the air. But his will had become suddenly heavy and no flight could come. Astonished, he sat winded on the water-filled road, fairy voice and certainty on the one side and the silvery floating shawl on the other.

So, here was an unexpected dilemma: seek the safety of the burrow or follow the river in adventure? The silvery shawl was approaching a bend in the river beyond; soon it would be out of sight. Tom picked himself up, bottom wet, and ran along the bank.

The water flowed quickly carrying the shawl merrily along, trapping bubbles in the gossamer loops. The river wound through rushes dividing itself in two to pass tiny islets and finding itself on the other side. Meanwhile, Tom ran along the bank path. He was happy. He breathed in the sweet air of the fresh running water as he chased the shawl. Motion suited him. Running was a novelty and an adventure. His unconscious laughter echoed the giggling river.

Unknown to the fairy boy he was being watched, as was the shawl. Circling above the river a grey bird with long grey wings, long lean legs, and a long yellow beak was eyeing both. With a squawk, the tall bird landed suddenly in the water trapping the shawl underfoot and forcing it down into the riverbed. The shawl sunk, drowned. Air bubbles rising from the pressure of the bird's intent, ebbed quickly away.

The Heron eyed Tom silently. Tom reached automatically over his shoulder for an arrow with which to fell the fiendish river bird, but none were there.

"You are far from your home – boy."

Tom nodded.

"This is a dangerous place for a child like you – anything could happen. Anything could catch you, could eat you."

"Please sir, please let me have the shawl."

"So that is what you chase? It must be of extreme importance for you to leave your lands."

Tom stood still and straight, refusing to answer, refusing to move. Seconds passed, minutes. How long could the feathered statue stand still in the water? How long could a fifteen-year-old fairy boy, whose muscles only knew motion, be the bird's reflection?

Eventually, the heron lost interest and lifted his leg allowing the Queen's shawl to rise to the surface and race relieved away.

Tom too raced. He ran from the bird, pursuing the spider's web shawl, but now with an unwelcome nervousness in his breast. His anxiety rose as the path drew silently away from the river until the two courses were separated by an expanse of rushes. Tom strained to see the shawl – yes, a glimpse here and there, the light reflecting on the bubbles caught in the delicate threads.

Soon the path returned to the waterside and Tom saw that on its journey turquoise bright kingfisher feathers had looped themselves between the bubbles and the pearls. The Fairy Queen's shawl seemed to have been transformed into a strange and beautiful water creature. Tom pressed on following the shady path until voices caught him short. There ahead on a rickety wooden bridge two fishermen rested watching the river and their rods.

"Please don't let them see it," Tom's lips willed in silence.

Too late, the older one was already recasting his line while calling,

"Jimmy, stir your stumps and help me."

Jimmy duly reeled in to recast and catch the trout of exceptional size and unusual colour, but not being as swift or as careful as his partner only succeeded in entangling the one line with the other permitting the silver shawl to continue its journey uninterrupted under the bridge and out from the woods.

Relieved, Tom ran on, the disappointed arguments of the two fishermen hiding the sound of his running feet beating loudly on the pebbled path. Reaching the edge of the woods, Tom was once again stopped in his tracks, not now by danger but by beauty. Never before had his eyes beheld such splendour. Could such a place as this exist outside the realms of fairyland?

Losing its speed the river had now widened out to a gracious lake from which smooth green hills rose gently to the blue skyline. On the far side of the lake, a Palladian bridge kissed the river adieu and watched it ribbon to the boundary of the park. Overseeing the magnificent, peaceful vista was a house grander than any Tom could have imagined.

The pearly kingfisher shawl drifted languidly across the mirror lake, as if taking time to admire the picturesque landscape. Tom reached the water's edge and strode purposefully into its cold depths glad that he had finally reached the end of his quest. But his shoes were no longer butterfly light, they were the weight of the real world and dragged him down. Bubbles swiftly filled his bulging shirt giving him buoyancy but not speed.

Bedraggled and disappointed, Tom abandoned the rescue. There was no chance of retrieving the shawl from the bridge as the walls were too high and the banks beyond were too steep. He would have to risk leaving the waterside to follow the path around the house to where, his instinct told him, the two would re-join beyond.

The spider's web shawl continued its journey alone, catching sunlight in its gossamer loops which the water then wove between the bubbles and the pearls. The river had created a garment of exceptional beauty and enjoyed its creation, leading it to the Millpond. There the water added lily petals, pink and white, to the bright blue feathers and let the shawl float dreamily among the lily leaves, bathing in the lemon fragrance until it reached the mouth of the mill. Here it became trapped in the mill teeth and here it waited.

"Papa, come quickly, you must come quickly," an urgent voice called. "Papa, please a bird is caught in the grate, please help."

The miller took a long stick kept for the purpose and rescued the shawl lifting it high into the air and depositing it in the hands of his delighted daughter.

Not a bird but a shawl – a beautiful, shining, sparkling water shawl. The little girl's eyes were wide with wonder.

"Papa, a fairy shawl, a real fairy shawl. Oh may I keep it, may I, please?"

The father's face softened with love for his child. He did not earn the money to give her much. He nodded. He knew it was not a fairy shawl and that whoever had lost it upstream would never arrive to claim it.

Laughing in joyous pleasure the little girl wrapped the Queen's shawl around her slight shoulders and over her thin cotton dress and felt herself to be as beautiful as a fairy princess.

Tom watched all from the river's edge. His youthful limbs demanded action. He should creep into the mill house and steal the spider's web shawl. But his growing good sense held him still. He watched the little girl swirling beside the water chatting merrily to her imaginary fairies, wearing his Fairy Queen's shawl. And as he did so, he knew what he should do. He knew without a doubt what she would do, his gentle, generous Queen. So with new maturity for his soon to be sixteen summers, he turned silently away and followed the river home to his fairyland pool.

13.

OXBLOOD

Her sobs are smothered by the winter rain — suffocated. Clumsily, desperately she works the heavy garden gate latch, the cold numbing her hands. She runs, stumbling, fearful, scrambling up the muddy lane to get away, to reach somewhere else, to reach a place of safety. But there is no safety. A haunted cry far off in another world marches relentlessly upon her, nearer and nearer, bearing down on her. She is guilty. The icy rain in the lane stones her weary flesh. The cry is upon her. The cry is a scream. The scream grips her by the breast, by the hip. It takes her by the shoulders and shakes her until eyes wide open, she stares into the dark silence, her heart pounding to break her ribs and burst out of the confines of her chest cavity to shatter on the mat-less floor.

"I can't say you'll be happy here, Ruth," Mrs Evans had said to her when she showed Ruth to her attic bedroom. "No one here is exactly happy. But I'll do my best to look out for you and no matter what, I expect high standards of attention and cleanliness. There will be no village slovenliness in any house under my care."

"Yes, Mrs Evans," Ruth replied, confused. Mrs Evans seemed kind and when Ruth looked at her she thought of a dandy-lion clock, her grey hair soft and round pinned up carefully at the back of her head, decorated appropriately with a lace morning cap, her dress woven greys trimmed with a discreet lace collar. Sturdy as a dandy-lion holds tall, refusing to be dug up, but fragile, its clock seeds spread to the wind in a single breath. But her words were just as mysterious as Ruth's mother's had been.

"Be a good girl, work hard, and makes sure only those that notice you are those that should," her mother had said as she embraced Ruth and watched her set out from the small child-filled cottage, her fledging adult daughter leaving the nest.

The autumn sun had only just woken up to kiss the scarlet Hawthorne berries as mothers kiss their rosy-cheeked babies. A robin redbreast kept Ruth company along the lane, sharing incomprehensible gossip that the girl could not return. She carried her breakfast – a slice of her mother's bread, a small bundle of her clothes and her book, her well-worn copy of *The Pilgrim's Progress*.

Ruth breathed in the mild chill of September's fresh morning enjoying the sensation of the cool air on her skin. It was like the deep waters of the stream by the brick bridge where she splashed with playfellows before her mother uttered the word 'modesty'.

"How old are you again, child?" Mrs Evans asked

"Sixteen, if you please."

"Be sure to work alongside Betsy," Mrs Evans continued, "and…" she paused, "best to keep your bedroom door locked."

For a moment the young woman and the older beheld together the iron lock on the inside of Ruth's attic door.

September ripened to October. The Master and the Mistress were away in the North Country, shooting on friends' large estates. Ruth was careful with her tasks and earned Mrs Evans' pleasure. Betsy laughed when she showed Ruth how to clean the copper so it shone so bright the two servant girls could see their faces reflected in its glory, burnished halos around their hair as if they were God's angels.

"Go on with you, Ruth," her laughter settled to a sigh, "there ain't nothing angel-like around here."

The carriage arrived with a clatter on the cobbles. The household had been toiling as black ants in preparation and now the whole staff stood in readiness to greet and be inspected. The Mistress, pale and grey, retired immediately to her chamber, weary of her long journey no doubt. The Master descended at his leisure and greeted two prized hunting dogs, that came bounding to his side. He stood square surveying his property, from the ornate brick chimneys to the latticed windows, from Mr Rose the butler, the two gardeners, Mrs Evans, the cooks, and the maids – Betsy and Ruth.

Ruth wondered what he was like, this broad-shouldered man. What kind of master would he be? And she looked at him. She looked straight at him. And he noticed her.

"Lower your eyes," Betsy hissed from the corner of her mouth, grabbing Ruth's wrist silently and holding it tight, their hands obscured by their dark skirts.

To begin with, he never spoke. He watched her. He looked at her. She didn't raise her eyes to his again.

One morning he found her. He found her alone. The breakfast room was cold and dreary begging for a hearty fire to toast the Mistress when she rose. Ruth was kneeling over, bending down into the grate to clean the ash when she felt him close behind her. He had approached noiselessly, a cat hunting a mouse. She dared not move. He put his hand on her shoulder and she flinched away.

"Ruth — stay where you are," he whispered into her ear as he placed his right hand over her breast, cupping the flesh through her bodice, his oxblood signet ring glinting in the early morning sunshine. He moved his left hand to the apron of her waist, momentarily playing with the ribbon fastening before permitting himself to let it rove over her hip.

"You don't mind do you, Ruth — you would please your Master wouldn't you?"

He pushed himself against her back forcing her to clutch onto him to prevent herself from tumbling into the grate. She cried out.

"No sound — hussy," he hissed. She bit her lip so hard she could taste salt blood and trembled.

"Let me be," silent tears screamed.

An almighty clatter of metal resonated around the breakfast room. Betsy stood at the threshold, black coal soot settling on her clean white apron, scuttle and fire-irons at her feet as escaping coals rolled under the table chasing each other towards the mahogany side-board.

"Well, well," their Master turned to Betsy affably, as if welcoming a house guest to the breakfast table. "You'd better clear up the mess, girl," he added with a laugh as he left the room, passing Betsy stern and straight in the doorway her eyes on the fireplace and a sobbing bundle in the grate.

Betsy wiped the tears from Ruth's eyes and the blood from her lip.

"Now you know. We can never be alone." And together they cleared the coals from the floor so that by the time the Mistress took her breakfast nothing had happened. That night Ruth barricaded her chair to her locked bedroom door.

She worked in the shadows to be out of his view, but he watched her.

"Ruth, you are pale and thin," her mother fussed when she returned to her cottage for her half day's holiday, as she spread honey thickly on a slice of warm bread offering it to her daughter on her best plate of blue and white, an heirloom reputedly from Delft. She counted the money that Ruth had earned into a round, wooden snuffbox with a faded picture of a farm-hand forking hay, secreting it in the deep corners of the dresser. Did she know? Ruth nibbled the corner of her honey bread in silence.

Footsteps pressed the floorboards on the attic staircase so that they groaned on the other side of her locked door. A haunted cry from a far off world carried on the wind.

"Ruth, you are avoiding me," the Master cornered her on the first-floor landing as she carried the daisy painted washing pitcher from the Mistress's bedchamber. "Put the pot down and come immediately to the study," he commanded.

He observed her hesitation to flee, a frightened rabbit before the fox.

"Ruth," he pleaded, "I will not touch you – I promise."

Unwillingly compliant – she obeyed.

His dark study was his fox's lair. Aged oak bookcases grew on the walls, the lattice windows barred the weak December light from entering, dark green tapis covered the floor as if woodland were in the house, a red velvet armchair rested luxuriously beside the fire. He took her gently by his ring bedecked hand and lead her to the desk releasing her only to turn up the brass oil-lamp lighting his face in the gloom. Beside the lamp on his desk was her book, her possession, her *Pilgrim's Progress*.

"Ruth," he moaned, "you tempt me, why do you do this wicked, unfeminine thing to me?" He dropped limply into the chair at his desk and cradled his dark curls, the gold signet on his little finger gleaming, diamond winking in the oil lamplight.

Soundless words she whispered, tears falling, creeping away from him, fleeing the lair.

Her reflection in the hall looking-glass halted her flight. Her reflection mocked her. "Temptress," the mirror Ruth whispered scornfully. "Hussy," her reflection judged.

"No. It isn't true," the real Ruth in the hall whimpered in reply.

Mrs Evans appeared from nowhere,

"Ruth, come and help me, child." Mrs Evans beckoned the girl quickly to her parlour, where she bid Ruth polish the second best silver dinner service – twice.

The scream grips her, takes her by the shoulder and the waist, oxblood signet ring glinting, and shakes her until eyes wide open she stares into the darkness.

"You must leave," Betsy whispers as she sweeps the staircase and Ruth dusts the bannisters alongside her.

"I know."

He watches her. He touches her. He enters her bedroom and runs his fingers through her possessions while she works in the house where everything and every person is his property. The winter nights are long and days are short. There is no snow this year, only ice-cold rain, and the lanes flow with mud.

Something will happen. He knows it. Mrs Evans knows it. Betsy knows it. The alternate Ruth in the mirror knows it. Even the Mistress, who has now noticed her, knows it.

Eyes wide open she stares into the dark silence, her heart pounding to break her ribs and burst out of the confines of her chest cavity to shatter on the mat-less floor.

Shadows stand guard for her in her small attic room as she dresses by candlelight and prepares her bundle. She creeps onto the attic landing, her mouse feet making the floorboards moan as if the wind is wuthering in the eaves. Silently, she enters his bedchamber. His dark curls are asleep on the linen pillow. Noiselessly, she opens the ebony Indian box on his dressing table. She chooses the gold solitaire and the oxblood. Then she leaves.

Her sobs are smothered by the winter rain – suffocated. Clumsily, desperately she works the heavy garden gate latch, the cold numbing her hands. She runs, stumbling, fearful, scrambling up the muddy lane to get away, to reach somewhere else, to reach a place of safety. But there is no safety.

14.
CATCH ME IF YOU CAN!

"Say you'll be mine," he whispered urgently, passionately, pausing his hungry kisses only to utter the words, hardly waiting for the response, before pressing his lips against hers. Pulling her close to him, as if the embrace could make her part of himself forever.

"Yes, my love," she replied. Her loose brown curls floated past her neck and onto her shoulders. She caught hold of his broad workman's hands which traversed her waist and hips, fingers seeking to undo buttons and reach the smooth, warm woman-skin below.

"You know I will marry you," she whispered into his ear, nuzzling against his neck, seeking his collar bone with her lips.

"When?" he pressed in urgent hope.

"When you return — when you return."

Three months. This no man's land of numbness had held Trudy in its suffocating fist for three months. She looked at herself in the stainless steel bathroom mirror and was repulsed by the haunted reflection. Unsatisfying sleep had shaped the sockets of her teal blue eyes into elderly bruises. Crow's feet, the shorthand of a joyous nature, seemed to her to be more evidence of time melting into middle age than of happy memories.

"No wonder he couldn't bear the sight of me," she muttered bitterly. "What's the point?" she continued under her breath as she went through her skincare routine like an automaton. Could the Clinique counter legitimately be a lifeline? She asked herself absently.

Absently – absent. That was all that was left. Absence. How could not being there be *so* there? How could not being present create such presence? What did it matter what she looked like? What she wore? Who would care? Certainly not him! Jeans and a fleece would do – and lipstick, of course. Always lipstick – like clean knickers; and for an instant, the hint of a smile, formerly so sparkling, so irresistible, played on her now coral lips.

Half an hour later, she parked outside St Peter's church as usual. The picturesque monument was set a little apart from the heart of the village. It had been built in Victorian times, the old church from centuries before having burnt down when struck by lightning in a November storm remembered for generations. The immaculate graveyard with its clean headstones, trimmed borders, clumps of daffodils in the spring, and wild roses in the beds in the summer, was set within the confines of a wall and a wooden gate. She had never thought of entering, but she had often stopped by the gate to pay her respects to the dead. What did it remind her of? Yes, it struck her now – the English cemeteries in the Somme, the ones she had visited as a History undergraduate. A little piece of England for your final resting place – whichever little piece of you that was found, she thought grimly.

Trudy wondered which bits of her were where. Three months ago he had fractured her, exiting her life with no warning and for good, sending splinters of herself in multifarious directions. A disembodied Trudy. She saw herself for an instant in her dressing gown carrying her head on a silver platter, walking in the country lane beside the church in her slippers. How ridiculous! How disrespectful! She frowned at the glimmer of her smile.

"When I return," he repeated, holding her white-bloused shoulders, so that her face was almost level with his, and gazing wondrously into her velvet eyes, scarcely daring to believe that his merry angel had said "yes". Momentarily he was lost for words and for kisses.

"Yes, you goose," she repeated, teasing him, enjoying the power she had over him to steal his words. Pushing him playfully away she turned, picked up her long skirts, and ran from where they stood, in the shade of the elder tree, their special tree, their special place at the edge of the cornfield at the plateau's ridge, and headed off down the hill. As she ran she called over her shoulder,

"Catch me if you can!"

She was agile and speedy despite the stays. It was a hot day, but the trees at the edge of the field gave shade to her path as she ran, knowing that he would follow and knowing that he would catch her.

"Cassie, wait," he called, astonished that she had slipped from his embrace and was off like the wind, retracing her steps from not yet an hour before, in the direction of St Peter's church and the village.

"Four months," Trudy sighed as she turned off the ignition and withdrew the key, pocketing it in her fleece jacket. The daffodils in the graveyard were withered. "Like me," she thought grimly. She changed her shoes into her walking boots, balancing one foot in turn on the open boot of her car as she tied the complicated laces. The black carpet covering the boot floor was splattered with dust and blades of drying grass, remnants of all these walks that she clung to religiously in the hope that they were making her feel better, that nature was sapping her sadness, as they'd told her it would.

As she turned into the lane that ran alongside the church, a Labrador puppy bounded up to her, out with its owner for a walk. The paleness of its fur reminded her of the pale yellow petals of the late spring narcissi. She patted the puppy's head – absently. Not there. "Good boy – Good dog." She didn't even notice the dog's owner.

Jim caught her firmly in his strong arms, as she knew he would, both laughing. Small droplets of sweat gathered at the base of his neck about his blue necktie. By this time next year they would be married, she thought, maybe with a baby on the way. Her heart was full as she drew his sunburnt arm, with his shirt sleeves rolled up to the elbow, around her slim waist and wrapped her white bloused arm around his, to return thus entwined to the village through the fields and past the church and its graveyard – talking, planning for their future.

A different day, at last. A spring lightness had crept through her open window with the early morning sunshine and had touched her brow so that when she woke she did not feel so heavy. A more than 'just lipstick' day. A foundation and blusher day. A younger Trudy smiled back from the mirror.

The Labrador pup bounded up to her again on the path beside the church.

"He knows you now," laughed the pleasant voice of his owner.

Trudy bent to fuss the dog, patting it gently between the ears as she told him softly what a good boy he was, what a good dog. The Labrador pup, bigger now than when she had first seen it, strained to examine her smell more closely. She stole the owner a shy glance. Previously, she had only nodded at his boots in her hesitant "Hello". She was surprised to see a youngish face, although his mousey hair was thinning slightly.

"Funny, I thought from his boots he was old," she said to herself, and blushing at her daftness and embarrassed by her unsociability, she hurried on.

Today was a different day. She breathed the late spring air, inhaling fully the purple scent of a thousand or more woodland bluebells. The aroma of spring was a liqueur thawing her senses and her body. Instead of keeping her eyes fixed on the stony path and rutted ridges of the ploughed fields, now dusted with shoots of green, she raised her eyes and saw a skylark swoop and dive in the blue, with an urgent, desperate song. Beyond, on the skyline was a lone elder tree calling her up, up to the top of the hill to the plateau's ridge.

So she answered the call, her senses yearning for the freedom of the summit and the view of what could be.

"Catch me if you can!" a happy voice echoed along the path and Trudy heard the heavy breathing of two runners and two pairs of feet on the field-side path. She waited for the voice and the runners to appear. But they did not. Absence. No. Probably they had gone in the other direction, out of sight, beyond the purple carpeted woodland.

"No!" Cassie screamed as the shell of grief exploded in her soul and pulled her into a whirling vortex of fractured time and sense. The black-edged letter to his family, containing words from his Officer that she could hardly take in, words such as 'loss', 'bravery', 'died a gentleman', tumbled to the floor, where his broken father stooped to pick it up.

"No," she sobbed. Huge body-engulfing, physical sobs which relentlessly pounded at her body, proving that she lived and was whole, while his body, containing her heart and her future, lay in pieces in a muddy French field.

"No!"

The golden corn swayed in the summer breeze. Trudy traced the steps of the lovers around the fields and up to the summit.

"Catch me if you can!"

She had never seen them, but she knew they were there, hearing their echoing feet and happy laughter. She wasn't afraid. She liked the trace of love. It fitted with the growing corn, the hatched fledglings, the swelling blackberries. A time for all seasons – now where had she heard that before?

At the summit of the hill, under the old elder tree, she looked up to the soaring skylark, closed her eyes, and allowed the August sunshine to bathe her tanned face with the fulfilling warmth of summer. The air was thick and drowsy and the birds sang lazily to her in the trees.

Was that a blackbird?

No, it was a sob.

Trudy sensed the crying woman beside her under the elder tree.

"He's dead. He's gone. I want to die with him," Trudy heard in the elder's whispering leaves.

The woman was so close that Trudy could have reached out to touch and comfort her, except that the chasm of time between them was an unbreachable eternity. Trudy stood in the sunshine, her eyes shut yet extending the arms of her soul to console this grieving, unknowable woman.

The sobbing softened and turned away. Instinctively, Trudy followed down the hill, through the fields, past the woodland. Ahead of her, she saw the woman; her loose brown curls floating over her white blouse, her long brown skirts catching in the dry summer grass, as she made her way to the church and the graveyard – to the quiet corner of England.

Trudy followed her into the graveyard, crossing the threshold she had never passed before. She stopped in front of a row of carefully tended graves, and waited, for what, she didn't know. A soft wet nose nuzzled against her left hand and licked her fingers. She stroked his narcissi pale head absently – presently.

"We'll never know who she was," the owner's voice said to the right of her.

Trudy did not turn to acknowledge his presence and instead gazed around at the headstones; so many names, so many dates. Had life for this woman stopped in 1915 when the shell exploded, shattering her heart and her future, or had her heart mended, had a new future been created with a headstone date of 1965, 1975, 1985?

"So you saw her too?" Trudy asked.

"From time to time, depending on the season."

"Catch me if you can," Trudy whispered softly, respectfully, as her eyes scanned the Victorian church, the war memorial with the name, perhaps, of the woman's lover, the gravestones, and the lane alongside, before turning, at last, to smile at her companion.

"I'm Nick," he introduced, "and this is Max," he said, petting his dog alongside him.

Postscript: The ripe, lush blackberries were so satisfying to share, Trudy mused, as she dropped a handful into the ice-cream tub he was holding out for her hedgerow collection. And she smiled as she popped the juiciest into his mouth, while the narcissi-furred dog foraged at his master's feet.

15.

BUTTERFLY MEMORIES

"So did you manage to get all of the fence put up in the end?" Philip asked his friend, Jeremy, as he bent down to tie up his walking boots. Jeremy, whose boots were already done up, replied,

"Yes, Mark came round with the grand-children and helped me get the last posts in."

"Was the fencing expensive?"

"No, I got the panels for a good price from the garden centre."

"Did they deliver?"

"Yes, it was easy as pie."

Boots tied up securely, Philip stood up straight and locked his four by four which they had come in together, pressing the button on his key. The two friends started to walk away from it along the lane.

"I'm thinking of replacing the fence at the end of the garden. It's in quite a bad state," Philip mentioned as they passed the old white cottage and turned off onto a path along the side of a field.

Philip and Jeremy had walked this route many times before. They hardly needed to concentrate on directions, their feet just seemed to lead the way, leaving them free to chat and admire the ever-changing beauty of their countryside. When they had first met they had not been what you call real friends; they had not had that much time – their children were young and they both worked long hours, Philip in PR and Jeremy in engineering. That had changed when Jeremy's twins Mark and Fiona and Philip's daughter Rachel had grown up and moved away. At about the same time, Philip and Jeremy found that they had reached a comfortable plateau in their corporate worlds, and took their feet off their respective career ladder accelerators. It was probably Philip who had first suggested that they go for a walk while their wives had coffee, but it could have been Jeremy. When they had both retired, only a few years ago, they had found that despite the almost obligatory charity and committee work that they both were now involved in in the community, they nevertheless had ample time to enjoy each other's company and roam the Hertfordshire footpaths. Their wives thought it was good for them and left them to it.

"You know that large cherry that was unhappy last year?" Jeremy asked.

"Yes?"

"It seems to have died, no leaves or blossom. It's going to have to come out. Can you give me the number of your tree-man?"

As they chatted, Philip and Jeremy followed the path along the edge of the field. The set-aside, the area at the edge of the field where crops had not been planted, was a weedy garden of Eden; lush green nettles with jagged leaf edges jostled for space with nettle sisters, ballet dancers in their cream petal tutus; tall elegant Queen Anne's Lace – a magnet for butterflies and bees; green alkanet with clusters of bright blue flowers; clumps of pale forget-me-nots, and bluebells, seeded by the wind, far from their bluebell families.

Up ahead, the path turned 90 degrees to the right and skirted around the top edge of the field to a stile. As they approached the bend, the friends saw that there was a man ahead of them. He was walking quickly and with purpose towards the stile. When he arrived, he stopped and looked at the wooden planks closely. Then he resolutely turned his back on it and walked quickly away, retracing his steps. He had almost reached the end of the path, to the point where it would turn 90 degrees to the left and would lead him straight into Philip and Jeremy, when he stopped, looked all around himself – at the trees, the field, the sky, the grass at his feet. Then he hastily turned 180 degrees and made his way back to the stile.

Philip and Jeremy had both noticed the man and said nothing. Perhaps he was lost.

The man reached the stile for a second time. But again he stopped and looked like he hardly knew what to do with it, like he hardly knew how to climb over it. He turned his back on it again and this time scurried, as rabbits do to find cover, to retrace his steps back to the 90-degree bend, whereupon again he stopped dead in his tracks.

"Something's not right here," Jeremy said quietly, observing the strange progress of the man up ahead.

Phillip took matters in hand, as he always did. The man now stood exactly at the 90-degree bend, looking first to his left and then to his right, then to his left again and then again to his right. He took no notice of the two walkers making their way towards him.

The man was tall and lanky. He had a neat grey beard and moustache and neat, short grey hair. He wore good walking boots, a long-sleeved navy top, and a khaki lightweight gilet. He carried a small backpack on his shoulders.

"Hello there," Philip greeted the man, his face wide and cheerful, his voice full of easy warmth.

"Hello," the man replied cautiously, revealing uncertain eyes behind the lenses of his glasses.

"Are you alright?" Philip continued.

"I think I'm a bit lost," the man replied.

"Where do you want to go?" Philip asked.

"I'm not really sure," the man answered.

"Where have you come from?" Jeremy asked kindly.

"I come from Dorset," the man replied, eyes lighting up. "Do you know it?"

Philip and Jeremy exchanged glances in which they both sought to see if the other thought the same as himself; that the stranger they had met needed their help.

"Do you want to go home?" Jeremy asked the man.

"Yes, yes, I think I do."

"Do you know where your home is?" Philip asked. It seemed a little rude to ask this, he knew, and in asking the question he felt that he was being condescending, talking to an adult as if he were a child, but the comment about Dorset did not fill Philip with much hope that this confused man knew where he lived.

"Of course I do!" The man replied, shocked at the question. "It's a redbrick house on a windy road."

Philip and Jeremy stood on the path, racking their brains to think of a redbrick house on a windy road that could be nearby. It was just possible that he meant the row of cottages on the road into Sandridge, which was not too far from where the three of them were standing by the set aside at the edge of the field.

"We'll have to try and get him home," Philip whispered to Jeremy. Jeremy nodded in agreement and tried to get the man to tell them more about his home, to see if the man could remember anything else that could help them identify where he lived – a road name, a house number, near a farm, near a school.

"Perhaps he has a phone?" Phillip suggested.

He did not have a phone. In fact, he seemed utterly perplexed why his new acquaintances thought he should have a phone, when phones are in houses, not fields. There was a chance that there was a clue to his identity, maybe even his address in his backpack, but the man's body became tense with anxiety when they suggested that they look inside it. There was nothing for it, but to make for the cottages on the road to Sandridge. Either this would be where the man lived, or at least it might be somewhere for him to wait while they contacted the police.

The quickest way to the cottages was to follow the field around and cross over the stile. However, when the man reached it, as before, he was quite unable to place his hands on the pole, raise his foot onto the step and swing his leg over. He stood perfectly still, viewing the stile with suspicion and fear. Philip demonstrated how to climb over the wooden structure; climbing up, swinging his bottom over slowly. Jeremy said he would take the man's weight and guide him across, but the man would not move. It was as if the stile was an unbridgeable hole in his head. It would never be crossed. There was nothing for it but to take him the very long way round, all the way back along the route that Philip and Jeremy themselves had taken to reach this point.

The incident with the stile depressed them both. How terribly sad, to forget where you live, to forget how to do something as simple as climbing over a stile. Jeremy's thoughts wandered to his father. How day by day, especially towards the end, the strong man whom he had loved had become a fainter and fainter version of himself, like when a child rubs out a pencil drawing, until only the frailest hint of an image, of what had been, remains on the paper.

Abandoning the stile, however, raised the lost man's spirits. He might not remember where he lived, but he could remember his name, it was Howard and he could remember the names of all the butterflies fluttering over the set aside; admirals, tortoiseshells, peacocks, and commas. More than once he almost dived headfirst into the nettles in his enthusiasm to examine a butterfly up close. He was equally excited by the birds, commenting to his rescuers on the songs he could hear, identifying thrush and the warblers in the hedgerows.

When they reached Philip's car, Howard was quite content to accept a lift to the row of cottages that the friends suspected was where he came from.

"*This* is where I live," Howard cried out brightly when Philip pulled up in the road outside the cottages.

"Will there be anyone in?" Jeremy asked, beginning to worry that there still might be problems if no one was there, if Howard didn't have a key in his bag, or didn't remember that he had a key in his bag, since he was not going to allow them to look in it.

"Oh yes!" Howard confirmed with great assurance. "There's a woman who lives there. She's always there. She'll let me in."

The car had scarcely drawn to a halt before Howard was fumbling with the car door, trying to get out. He bounded up the drive of the middle cottage and rang on the doorbell.

It was an attractive cottage with a rose trained around the door and porch, reaching up to the first-floor window. Any day now the buds would burst into butter-yellow glory. The front path was lined with lavender and sedum. A buddleia bush thrived by the gate. The cottage garden was a butterfly haven.

The door was opened by a grey-haired woman wearing jeans and a fleece.

"Hello, Howard," she smiled. "Have you had a nice walk?"

"Oh yes, I have, I really have," Howard replied and he hurried into the house, not even turning around to thank Philip and Jeremy for bringing him home.

The lady smiled affectionately at him and was about to close the door when she noticed Philip and Jeremy on the path. Momentarily she was confused, she wondered what two strange walkers were doing in her garden.

"Hello," Philip smiled in his usual warm way. "We found Howard and brought him home," he explained.

The woman's face fell instantly. Jeremy realised how in a matter of seconds her agile features had changed from affection to confusion to disappointment.

"Thank you," she said softly, "I appreciate that, it was good of you."

"Is he alright?" Philip asked, pushing for a reason for the strange behaviour, seeking confirmation of his suspicions.

"My husband's memory isn't what it was," she explained with a lump in her throat.

"Do you think he should be out by himself?" Jeremy asked as gently as he possibly could.

"Yes, I do," she answered sincerely. "The exercise is good for him. He loves walking in the fields. It makes him happy. When he can't remember how we live in this house or even who else lives in this house," she added with a twinge of bitterness, "he remembers everything that lives in the fields."

They thought of the butterflies and the birds, of how Howard had nearly tumbled into the nettles to reach them, how his eyes were bright, how he knew all their names, even the Latin ones.

"But maybe he should have someone with him?" Philip questioned, equally gently, not wanting to criticise the wife for letting her dementia suffering husband roam, but thinking that he ought to make the point that perhaps it wasn't safe – after all he and Jeremy had had to rescue him.

"I don't know how much longer he will be able to do it by himself, but for the moment we have to keep trying, every day we have to keep trying," she said wearily, sounding as if it were a message for herself as well as for her husband. "Thank you for helping him," she repeated and moved to close the door and encourage the walkers to go.

"We're glad we could help."

"We'll keep an eye out for Howard when we walk round here."

"Thank you, I appreciate that," she replied, and she closed the door on them to continue caring for her husband.

PART 3: TOWNS
HATFIELD

16.

GUNS FOR MOSQUITOS

It was just as if nothing had changed, and yet everything was somehow different.

Ronald had dozed on and off during the journey down the A1M from Newark as he sat in the front passenger seat next to his great-granddaughter, Annabel, who was driving. Her boyfriend, Leigh, sat folded into the back seat behind her. Ronald couldn't make out anything that the young man said from his position in the rear and after a few times asking, "What did you say?" he had given up even trying to hear and had found dozing an easier way to pass the miles.

"We're here, Great-Grandad," Annabel had said, as she flicked the indicator and turned off the motorway, doubling back on herself to pick up the Great North Road, the old A1.

Ronald opened his eyes and instantly knew where he was. He recognised the fall then the rise of the road. He saw signs to familiar place names. When he had lived here there had been no road signs, as directions had been removed to confuse the Germans should they invade. The road was familiar, but dissimilar to the one that he remembered. Houses had sprung up in the years since he had last travelled back and forth on it during the few months that he had been posted in Hertfordshire in the war.

The road curved ahead of him and he saw castle-like St John's church at the head of Lemsford village in its familiar place on the road's bend.

"Nearly there now," Annabel updated her passengers as her car passed the church.

Ronald strained to his left to look out at the fields. In his mind's eye, he could see the gun emplacement and all its attendant activity. Now there seemed to be nothing but an unidentifiable arable crop and hedges.

"Here we are, Great-Grandad," she said as she signalled into the car park of the Crooked Chimney pub. "I bet you're ready for your lunch!"

Ronald was relieved. He needed a pee and his legs were cramped. He felt tired already but was determined not to be. His daughter, Susan, had opposed the trip, saying that he was too old, he couldn't cope, she couldn't see the sense in wanting to go back, it was unimportant, an unnecessary waste of time and energy. But his obstinacy and Annabel's ethereal calmness had triumphed, and now that he was here, back at Lemsford after all these years, he so wanted Susan to be wrong. This journey was not a waste of time. It was not unimportant. To him.

Leigh unfolded himself quickly and leapt out of the car to open the door for his girlfriend's elderly relative.

"Thank you," Ronald croaked in his old man's wobble, pleased to see that this younger generation knew their manners despite what some of the folk his own age grumbled. He made for the gents with his head held as erect as he could and only lightly relying on his walking stick.

When he had finished his business he found the youngsters sitting at a table near the window. There were two pints and a small glass of something clear and fizzy on the table.

"I've bought you a pint," Leigh said. "I thought you'd like the local brew."

"Thank you," Ronald answered, wondering whether he would be wise to down all the brown liquid when he intended to spend the afternoon in a field where there was not likely to be a lavatory.

"Has it changed much, Great-Grandad?" Annabel asked.

Ronald looked around the pub. It was almost completely different, in every aspect apart from the layout. A middle-aged woman with short bleached hair was pulling pints behind the bar. She wore dangling earrings through the fleshy lobes and shining loops and studs which extended the whole way to the top of her ear, through the stiff gristle. Eighty years or so ago the neat and ordinary Earnest Brown had presided in her place. Today, the tables were occupied by groups of friends out for lunch, some probably from close by and others, like them, from further afield. Whereas when he had drunk here regularly, the customers had been soldiers and inhabitants of close by cottages. Even the name of the pub was different, then it had been 'The Chequers', now it was 'The Crooked Chimney'.

"Quite a bit, love," he replied.

A waitress, a young Chinese woman, in tight black jeans and a stiff white blouse, displaying her name 'Kelly Wu' on a badge at her breast, came to their table to take their food order. He found her hard to hear because she spoke in such soft tones, and he had to rely on Annabel to help him. He chose shepherds' pie with extra carrots and hoped he would have room for the sticky toffee pudding and custard.

"Have you come far?" Kelly asked Annabel, recognising that her accent was not local.

"We're down for the day from Newark, but Leigh's from round here," she explained. "We've come because my great-grandad was based here in the war."

"What the second world war?" Kelly said with surprise, looking closely at Ronald and registering that he must not just be old, but very old. "I didn't know there was much of the war going on here."

"Yes, Great-Granddad manned the guns which defended the aircraft factory at Hatfield where they used to make Mosquito aeroplanes. He says the guns were in the fields between here and the church."

"No way!" the waitress responded. "I never knew that. There's nothing there now," and she left to take the orders to the kitchen.

Ronald ate his lunch as quickly as he could, squeezing in the pudding and leaving most of the pint. Much as he was pleased to have returned to one of his old haunts, he wanted to go back to the field, to see again where it had all happened.

Annabel drove them as close to where her great-grandfather could remember the emplacement being as the road would allow. She eyed the track which they would now have to take warily, wondering if her great-grandfather could manage it. It had rained recently and puddles had gathered in the furrowed clay troughs in the path. If he should trip and fall and hurt himself she would be in deep trouble with her grandmother, Susan. Leigh, sensing Annabel's unease, offered Ronald his arm as support.

Kelly was right, there was no longer any sign of the war in the field. All traces of it had been manually moved, erased by time, grown over year after year with each season's crops.

"We had a gun there," Ronald stopped to say to Leigh, pointing with his stick at the empty field. "And another there. The ammunition was stored over there," he pointed to another corner of emptiness. "And just over there, that's where we camped – there weren't any huts, just canvas for us boys."

It seemed incredible that the whole encampment should have just disappeared. Back then there had been concrete roads along which to move the heavy guns and the ammunition supplies. They had lived and worked for months in this field and now there seemed to be no evidence at all of their presence. Just as the encampment had sprung up overnight, it had disappeared equally quickly when the need for the big defence guns had passed. The activity of war had disappeared from both sight and memory.

The crop, whatever it was, was poking through the ground, grassy shoots emerging enthusiastically from the red-brown mud. The fields were larger than when he had been based here. Many of the hedges where he had seen thrushes and yellowhammers, blackbirds and robins build their nests that spring and early summer of 1940 had been ripped out to make larger spaces for larger machinery to do their work. Once, in the peace of the afternoon when war forgot to be present, he had seen a fox cub under the hawthorn rim of the field, staring nervously at him with keen dark eyes, before disappearing, in an instant, to safety away from the unknown khaki creature standing only on two hind legs in the field before him.

"Did you shoot down any German planes?" Leigh asked impressed with the old man's contribution to history. His great-grandmother was going to be one hundred soon. She must undoubtedly have some wartime memories. He must try to remember to ask her.

The unpredictable spring wind picked up and pushed around Ronald's arms and legs. It toyed with a stray strand of his silver hair.

"Did you shoot down any German planes?" he heard Leigh ask.

He shivered.

"Are you okay, Great-Grandad? This wind's a bit cold isn't it?" Annabel worried, thinking perhaps they shouldn't linger too long in this exposed field.

"No worse than it always was out here, love," Ronald answered.

"Did you shoot down any enemy planes, Ronald?" Leigh asked again, more loudly, assuming Ronald couldn't hear.

It had happened early in the morning in the first week of October. The Battle of Britain was raging desperately in the skies. He was on duty that morning and had woken from a noisy night as the dew glazed the grass. The heavens were cloud-filled. An autumn mist seemed determined to cling to the fields despite the sun fighting to break through and burn it off. He had taken his position that morning at the emplacement alongside his fellow gunners, almost with enjoyment at the dank rural beauty so different from the northern town where he had spent all his life until the opportunity of war gave him unsought experiences.

Then, on the horizon, a plane appeared. The hazy, dawning sun, low in the sky, turned it to a dark bumblebee.

"One of our lads coming home," Gunner Hastings had said raising his binoculars to his eyes to observe the low flying craft more closely.

"Glad he's safely back," Ronald had replied. "It's a murky morning to fly."

There were no other planes in the sky.

Suddenly, the low bumble bee sound over Hatfield, no more than three miles away, changed its vibration. The whole of Gunner Hastings' body turned rigid.

"My God. It's a Jerry plane!"

In a split second, peace in the field had turned to battle. Orders were issued, decisions made, but the enemy plane was too low for a strike to be a success and in any case, it had turned.

Gunner Ronald Gissing and his gun team were ordered to load and fire, sending noise and power into the blue, in too late a gesture of defence.

"Jerry's coming back," Hastings shouted.

The Junker 88, its opportunity for destruction not relinquished, returned and shed its explosive load onto the De Havilland factory at Hatfield. The Light Anti-aircraft guns at the perimeter of the airfield caught off their guard at the plane's reconnaissance were ready for its return and struck the enemy with fire which lit the sky. The Junker limped away, flames blazing in its wake, and crashed into a field not many miles further north. Twenty-one factory workers lost their lives that day, seventy more were wounded.

"No, we didn't shoot down any planes, not here," Ronald replied.

He wished he had. He had always wished he had. Twenty-one people might have had long, happy lives as he had done. If only the plane had been higher in the sky. If only the weather had been brighter and they could have seen the plane more clearly. If only they had not mistaken it as British. But standing here in the field, he could see that from this distance and at this angle, with the sun low as it had been that morning and in that mist, there was no way back then in 1940 without radar to assist them, that they could have known it was an enemy plane.

The old man's face was strained with old sadness. Annabel put her arm around him and hugged him.

He had been re-posted the month after, to Sidmouth of all places, and had never returned to Hertfordshire until this day.

"Have you seen everything you wanted to see, Great-Granddad?" she asked softly. "Leigh's Mum's invited us to tea in Welwyn Garden City. We can go there now if you're ready."

"Thanks, love," he answered gratefully. He was quite worn out now and wouldn't say no to a cup of tea in a comfortable armchair and perhaps even a little sleep.

17.

THE GIRL UNDER THE OAK

"I wondered when you were going to wake up."

Disorientated from her slumber, Chisom scrambled to sit upright and looked around confused. Her eyes darted in a daze from the oak tree to the blue sky above, from the grass she was sitting on, to the woman sitting beside her – who had not been there when she had shut her eyes. She pressed her hands down into the green blades beside her, so that they acted like roots, like the roots of the ancient, famous oak under which she was sitting. Her fingers pressing into the warm damp earth gave her the sensation of grounding herself. She had been feeling like an intruder all afternoon, more now that someone was addressing her in such an imperious way. Yet she also felt intruded upon. She had been completely and comfortably alone when she had sat down under the tree and had stretched herself out on the lush green and closed her eyes. She must have dozed off and the stranger had come alongside her, entering into her space beneath the oak as she had been sleeping. Sleep had made her vulnerable. At least it was a woman's voice and not a man's.

The speaker was young, perhaps in her early twenties, not much older than herself. In appearance, the two women could not have been more different. Chisom now sat sprawled across the grass and her denim shorts and sunflower coloured gypsy blouse covered very little of her dark limbs. The stranger, in contrast, sat stiffly, her back straight, legs demurely to the side, an open book on her lap, and every part of her body, except for her pale, sun-hidden hands and face, was covered in rich russet and cream fabric. Even the stranger's hair was covered modestly by a stiff headdress. It was strange clothing. She looked like an Elizabethan lady-in-waiting. Chisom concluded that this woman must be one of the actresses from up at the house taking part in the Tudor re-enactment for the visitors. King Henry VIII had been in the Old Palace, answering endless questions from the children about which wife he liked best. He seemed relieved when the occasional adult asked him for an opinion on Wolsey or Cromwell. He had tried to engage Chisom in historical conversation as she passed but she had avoided his inclusion by studying her leaflet guide.

"I like your hair – your beads look like raindrops," the woman observed, having become impatient at Chisom's silence.

Chisom reached instinctively to the crystal clear beads at the end of her braids. Now it would be impossible for her to stand up and walk away, now she would have to be polite in her turn, although, in honesty, she didn't want to be drawn into polite chit-chat.

"Thank you," Chisom replied. She could hardly say 'I like yours,' as the woman's hair was covered. Nor could she say, 'I like your dress,' because she didn't. There was an awkward silence as Chisom sought out an inane nicety. Her eyes rested on the book. The lady followed the direction of Chisom's gaze

"Can you read?" the lady asked her.

"Of course I can!" Chisom spat in indignation. She'd endured many negative comments in her not so long life, some deliberate, some inadvertent, both equally harmful, but never had anyone assumed that because she was black she couldn't read.

"Excellent." the lady replied, ignoring Chisom's burning outrage. "One can't always take it for granted that a woman can read."

"This is ridiculous!" Chisom shouted in her head. She burned to say something to this strange actress to take her down.

"I can't just read you know," Chisom said sarcastically. "I'm studying computer programming at the university."

Again the lady ignored Chisom's hostility. It was as if she simply didn't notice it.

"A woman, at a University, how interesting!"

"Lady, I don't know who you are, but you have some really weird ideas, there are plenty of women at university."

Chisom began to stand up, annoyed that her time under the oak had been ruined by this mad actress who was poking fun at her.

A cloud of regret passed over the actress's face.

"Please don't go. I'm sorry I didn't introduce myself, I assumed you knew who I am. I am Elizabeth."

"I'm Chisom," Chisom replied, and then cussed herself for being drawn into an introduction.

"I'm very interested, and I'd very much like to know — what is this 'computer programming' you speak of?" Elizabeth asked. "Is it difficult?"

"Not really, it's just learning a lot of different languages to get the computer to do what you want."

"So do you like languages?"

"Not especially."

"I do. I can speak Latin, French, Spanish, Italian, and Dutch."

"Lady, that's too much. No one speaks that many languages these days. Did you say Latin? Why on earth would you want to do that? And what do you need so many languages for, girl, everyone speaks English."

"Because I like languages and it pleased my father."

Finally, Elizabeth had said something Chisom could relate to — because it pleased her father.

Chisom's father was a conveyancing solicitor. Her grandparents had fled to England during the Nigerian civil war. Her grandfather, educated and hard-working in Nigeria, was misjudged as uneducated and lazy in England because of the colour of his skin. For the sake of his family, he had laid aside personal ambitions, working hard in a garage as a car mechanic to pay their rent. Her grandmother, equally educated, had taken work as a cleaner to put food on her family's table. Chisom's father, born shortly after his parents had arrived in London, embraced their aspirations and trained, willingly or not — his family never knew — in law, a perfect ticket to financial independence and middle-class respectability. He sent his daughter to the best school he could find and set her on the course which would consolidate the family's position in society.

"And did it?" Chisom asked in a tone distinctly more gentle than she had employed before.

"Did it what?"

"Please your father."

"I think so. It's hard to tell, I saw him so infrequently," Elizabeth said sadly.

"He passed then, I'm sorry," Chisom sympathised and then cussed herself again. This woman was an actress, pretending to be Princess Elizabeth mourning the death of her father King Henry VIII, who was still up at the house deflecting criticism from a generation who were profoundly more sympathetic to the plight of his wives and his children than anyone living at his time had been.

"You know lady, you can cut it with me. You don't need to keep acting, you're not at the house now," Chisom said, resuming her cutting tone of earlier.

"It would be more fitting if you addressed me as 'Princess Elizabeth' rather than 'lady'," Elizabeth said, a slight hardness entering into her voice.

Now Chisom had had enough. She picked up her handbag and Hatfield House leaflet and made to leave.

"I'm sorry you are leaving so soon," Princess Elizabeth said by way of apology. "I see so many people, yet so few are polite enough to speak to me."

She turned her rich dark brown eyes away from Chisom and looked out across the park in the direction of Hatfield House.

"They will come soon and then it will all be over, we won't be able to talk and there is so much I want to know."

There was an ache in the Princess's voice that was so real that Chisom felt it was an object that could be touched and not merely a feeling. She put her handbag and leaflet back onto the ground and decided to play along with this strange lady, what harm could it do?

"What do you want to know?"

The Princess's face lit up in expectation of a feast of knowledge about to be offered to her on a silver platter.

"How do you come to be here is my first question?"

"This is my last year at the university, I've been here 3 years and I've just taken my exams. I'll be going soon. I've got a job with a bank in London. I start in August. Every holiday when I went home my Dad would ask me if I'd visited Hatfield House. 'Why would I want to do that?' I'd ask him. 'Why would you *not* want to do it?' he'd say to me. Then I'd answer, 'Uni students don't go to country houses in their spare time, they sleep and go clubbing.' He didn't like it when I said that," Chisom chuckled as she reminisced. "'Don't you go sassing me young lady', he'd say wagging his finger and imitating grand-mummy, "Maybe you students should be taking some interest in your history," he would say to me. So I decided to visit before I left."

"You visited to please him then?"

"Yeah, I guess so. I felt really out of place looking around though – there were loads of old people and families. No one my age."

"And did you like the house? I have only ever seen it from the outside, I can remember the Old Palace very clearly."

"Yes I did, it's very beautiful. There are some paintings of you inside."

"Are there indeed?" The Princess leant slightly towards Chisom, eager to learn as many details from her as she could.

Chisom wished she had concentrated a little harder when she had looked around the house. She hadn't paid much attention to the detail, she had scanned the larger story; the function of the rooms, the colour of the décor. She thought back to the black and white marble hall where she had paused at the end because a group of visitors had gathered in front of the wall. They had been looking at a portrait of Queen Elizabeth that she remembered seeing before in history lessons at school before she had dropped all the arts subjects to focus on maths and computer studies.

"There's a really famous portrait of you in the Marble Hall called 'The Rainbow Portrait.'"

"Can you describe it?"

"You're wearing a gorgeous orange dress covered in little eyes and ears and you're holding a rainbow. You have pearl jewellery and there's a lot of lace, kind of all around you." She could not describe it any more eloquently and she kicked herself, for she knew her verbal portrait fell far short of the marvel of the real thing.

"How interesting," the Princess replied, listening intently. "I like how you have described that. How did I wear my hair?"

"It was loose."

"Like this?" the Princess asked, and she pulled off her head dress to reveal ginger-red locks wound around her head. She shook her head and the red glory tumbled down onto her shoulders, a fiery mane in the afternoon sunshine. Chisom gasped, taken aback by the splendour of it.

"I like your hair!" As with the portrait, her words did not seem to do justice to the marvel it was.

"Thank you," the Princess accepted the compliment with grace. "It won't be long now," she added.

"Until what?" Chisom asked, confused.

"Until they come."

"Who?"

"Sir William Cecil, Robert Dudley and their secretaries, two guards as well."

Chisom thought she had heard some of the names before. She thought she knew now what was going to happen. She thought she knew what message the men would bring.

"Here they come," the Princess said, nodding at a party of well-dressed men walking with intent across the park towards the oak tree, bearing the message that Queen Mary, her sister had died and that she was now Queen.

"What will you say to them?" Chisom asked.

"I will say, 'It is the Lord's doing and it is marvellous in our eyes.' I always do say that when they come."

"Don't you ever say anything different?" Chisom asked.

Queen Elizabeth looked surprised.

"There is no other response to be made. It is my destiny."

"But don't you sometimes think that it will be too much, that you won't manage?"

"I won't be Queen alone."

"Well you're not going to get married," Chisom said without thinking.

"No, I don't expect I shall," Queen Elizabeth said with gentle indifference.

Chisom felt embarrassed. It probably wasn't polite to tell someone what would not happen to them in their future. She tried to cover her mistake, digging into what she could remember of the Virgin Queen's life and reign.

"You didn't have much choice in men," Chisom said at last, slightly apologetically.

"You misunderstand me, Chisom," the Queen corrected. "I have the choice whether to govern alone or with the men I trust to advise me. I have the choice to work with the people's representatives in Parliament or to work against them. I have already decided. I will not govern alone."

The Queen wound her hair back around her head and replaced her headdress in readiness for the arrival of William Cecil and Robert Dudley and their entourage. She received the proclamation that she had heard thousands upon thousands of times before across the centuries and she repeated the words with which she always responded. Then she walked regally away, not alone, but surrounded by her advisors, leaving Chisom by herself beneath the ancient oak tree.

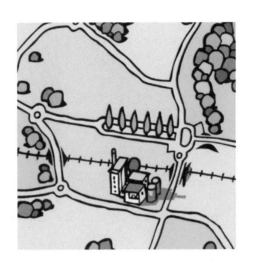

TOWNS
WELWYN GARDEN CITY

18.

THE MAN WHO TOOK HIS PIG FOR A WALK

21 -Lane
Welwyn Garden City
Hertfordshire
14th April 1982

Dear Esther

My Dad has a pig called Bertie. My Dad is a very busy man. He works hard in London all day, but when he comes home he likes to take Bertie for a walk in the woods where we live. Bertie is a very good and nice pig. Bertie would love to be on your tv show and so would my Dad.

From
Carrie Jones (age 9)

Carrie sucked the end of her HB pencil, wondering if she had written enough. She had already chewed through the red and black paint, exposing the soft, moist wood which encased the lead. The taste was soggy and comforting. She was pleased with her letter. She had written it in her best joined-up handwriting and she hadn't used any complicated words so she was confident that she had got all the spellings right. Bertie was a lovely pig. He had such cute little eyes. He deserved to be on the television. He was much more interesting than the silly Labrador puppy which could jump through hoops that Esther Rantzen had had on her show *That's Life* last week. Bertie liked to sunbathe. He liked to lie on his back and turn his tummy to the sun and wriggle in happiness making sweet little grunting noises. Maybe Esther would like to hear about that?

She wrote:

PS Bertie likes to sunbathe, but if he does that when he goes for a walk with my Dad it's a bit difficult becoz often Bertie likes sunbatheing so much he forgets how to walk and my Dad has to pritend to be a pig to show Bertie how to walk again.

There! That was a good letter. She was sure Esther Rantzen would want to have Bertie on her show. She put the letter into its envelope, licked the yucky glue paste to seal it, and then carefully wrote the address. It had been really difficult to copy down the address for *That's Life* from the tv screen without her parents noticing. She had had to do it over several weeks, memorising a line at a time and then rushing up to her bedroom to quickly write the line down before she forgot it. Carrie didn't have any stamps. She hoped her Mum wouldn't notice if she took a stamp from her purse. There were only 2 first class stamps, but there were 9 second class ones. She tore off 2 second class stamps as somehow 7 stamps looked closer to 9 stamps than 8 did. There was a post box at the end of their road. There would be no difficulty in posting the letter as she was always running along the road to play with her friend Joanna.

The Easter holidays finished and school started again for the summer term, but there was no reply from Esther. The Whitsun half-term came and went, but there was no reply from Esther. Carrie was disheartened.

"I can't believe Esther doesn't want you, Bertie," she said to the pig, tickling him between his ears. He loved that and moved closer to her legs to rub himself against her shins. "You'd be so good on the tv and so would Dad."

Carrie was sure her Dad would love to be on *That's Life*. The three of them watched it as a family every week. It was so funny. Her Dad roared with laughter. Sometimes her Mum would turn to her Dad and ask,

"Are you sure Carrie should be watching this, love?" and he would glance over at her and reply to her Mum,

"There's no harm in it, Bridget."

Carrie wasn't sure what her Mum meant. She must have been talking about the boring bits, which were, well – boring!

Recently, her Dad had been quite grumpy. It had started sometime after Christmas. He always got a bit cross with her when she left her Lego bricks in the hallway, but he had shouted so fiercely at her that she had cried and run to her Mum who had said,

"It's not her fault, Derek, don't take it out on her."

That probably wasn't the best thing that her Mum could have said, as they all ate their chicken pie dinner in silence that night. Often nowadays her Dad would sit still, staring into the distance, not concentrating on what was going on around him, and then he would jump up and call Bertie for a walk and the pair of them would head off up the road and into Sherrardspark wood. When she asked if she could go too, he didn't seem to hear and carried on walking.

"Don't worry about Daddy, he's tired, would you like to do a jigsaw with me?" Her Mum would ask.

"No, I wouldn't!" Carrie thought silently in her head. "I want to go for a walk with Bertie and Dad in the wood and I don't like jigsaws. I like Lego." She did say that once, before she wrote to Esther, but her Mum looked so wounded by her words that Carrie felt like crying, so now she just answered,

"Yes, that's a great idea Mum," at which her Mum would smile because she did like jigsaws. Then her Mum would say,

"We can take Bertie out by ourselves a bit later if you like if Daddy hasn't worn him out."

It was clear to Carrie that her Dad wasn't happy. It was also clear to Carrie that walking with Bertie in the woods made him happy and that watching *That's Life* made him happy. So the nicest thing she could possibly do for him was to persuade Esther to feature her Dad and Bertie on her show. She loved her Dad so much and she wanted him to be happy.

By June, Carrie had almost given up all hope of receiving a reply from Esther Rantzen. She couldn't understand why Esther or one of Esther's friends hadn't written back to her straight away. But then one morning the postman posted a letter addressed to her through their front door. There was another letter with an identical type-written address for her Dad. She opened the one addressed to her and read,

Dear Carrie

Thank you for your letter about Bertie and your Dad. We think that it would be great to have him on our show. We are going to write to your Dad to arrange it. We look forward to meeting you all.

Yours sincerely
Esther Rantzen

Carrie was elated. Dad wasn't in, so she ran straight out to Bertie in his pen in the back garden to tell him the good news.

Life had been good to Derek. He had a sunny disposition and he had free-wheeled through school. His A-levels hadn't been anything to write home about but he had the gift of the gab and landed a job in sales for a small window showroom in Colchester, the nearest large town to where he lived. As he had suspected deep down, he found that he was a born salesman, and he enjoyed being one. Work wasn't work when you got paid for it and it was fun. Soon the window showroom was too small for his abilities and he sought a promotion at an Essex based cleaning products company. The Essex girls were pleasant enough but Derek and his pals preferred to take the train into London to go to the nightclubs at Soho. This was where he met Bridget O' Farrell. He fell for her instantly, entranced by her silky black hair, soft porcelain cheeks, and accent so different and exotic to anything he knew. Luckily for Derek, Bridget was charmed by his flirtatious sales patter and agreed to meet him again, and again, and again, until she agreed to marry him.

Bridget had a job as a secretary in Aldgate, but she had no desire to carry on working when she had children. She wanted to stay at home and look after them. But she did not want that home to be a flat in Walthamstow, nor did she want to return to Ireland. Derek, for his part, felt that he had left Essex behind him. So when Bridget fell pregnant and the new little Jones family needed a house and a home, he set about finding one somewhere else. He studied the map of the South East of England and traced his finger along the train lines leading from the leafy counties into the great London termini until he found what he wanted for his family; a town in the countryside and on the mainline to the city.

He was now the Senior Sales Manager for a cosmetics company in central London. He managed dozens of portfolios, juggled clients. He embraced what every morning had to offer him, rising early and taking the train into Kings Cross, heading to the exciting bustle of the city. Sometimes he read reports as the train jostled him agreeably to work, sometimes he read a newspaper that he would buy at the station; *The Times, The Daily Mail, The Sun* – he didn't mind which, he read them more for the ads than the news content. Coming home every evening was a pleasure, leaving the dirty, busy capital and walking through the garden city central boulevard lined with roses in the summer and bulbs in the spring; home to where Bridget and Carrie waited for him. Each step he took away from the station was a step away from the stress of the day.

Both he and Bridget would have liked another child, but it was not to be. Soon a piglet, Bertie, joined Carrie in the family rather than a brother or a sister. She didn't seem to mind. Derek constructed a pen for Bertie in the garden but Bertie was scared alone outside and yelped and squealed. The sound upset Bridget so much that she brought her baby into the house, where he stayed until he decided of his own accord that he wanted to sleep in the pen. They found it was impossible to leave Bertie out of family life, and just as Bridget or Derek took little Carrie to play in the woods, Bertie came too, as if he were Carrie's little brother.

Derek liked to take Bertie out for walks alone, just the two of them. The paths in the wood twisted and turned through the glade of ancient hornbeam trees. Bertie would sniff and search the earth around the old trunks with his snout. Wherever the sun streaked onto the dirt path through the leaves and branches to form a pool of light on the ground, Bertie would launch himself into the golden puddle as if diving into a swimming pool, and roll onto his back to soak the sunshine into his soft flesh.

Derek needed these walks alone with Bertie more than ever this year. He had worked hard the previous autumn to secure a contract with a global cosmetic brand based in France. He had put in extra hours, briefed his team again and again, wined and dined everyone who counted. He was sure it was in the bag, but to his utter astonishment, they had given their business to another company. His chief executive was furious. For the first time in his life, Derek didn't know what to say. He couldn't explain what had happened. He had no words to describe his failure or the grey cloud that descended over his head and robbed him of joy and sunlight, that turned all his days into a chain of disappointment.

There was a brown envelope with his name and address typed on the front resting on the hall table when he came home from work. He stopped to look at it before taking Bertie out for their evening walk. He would have put the letter back on the table to open later except there was a BBC frank mark in the top right corner. He opened it and read,

BBC Studios
White City
London
7ᵗʰ July 1982

Dear Mr Jones

Your daughter has written to us about your pig Bertie and we would like to feature him on our programme in two weeks' time. If it is convenient for you we would like to come to Welwyn Garden City on 10ᵗʰ July at 10 am to film you and Bertie. We apologise for this short notice. Please telephone on the below number if you agree to be filmed and the time is convenient.

Yours sincerely
S. Draper assistant to C. Carr, editor of That's Life

Derek read the letter through once, he read it through twice. He felt sick.

"Carrie," he called out shakily. "Carrie, can you come down please?"

Bridget, alarmed by the choked tone of her husband's voice, poked her head out of the kitchen door.

"What's wrong, love?" she asked.

He handed her the letter which she read through once, and read then read through twice.

"Did you know anything about this?" he asked, the sick feeling in his stomach churning into anger.

"Of course not!" she defended her innocence.

"Carrie," they both called together. "Can you come down please?"

Carrie bounded out of her room and rushed down the stairs. She reached the bottom step and was halted in her tracks by the ferocious look on her Dad's face and the concerned look on her mother's.

"Carrie, did you write to That's Life about Bertie?" he asked her.

"Yes," she replied in a much littler voice than she wanted to.

"You shouldn't have done it, darling. You shouldn't have written without asking us," he said slowly, trying to contain his anger in syllables.

"But we all love That's Life – don't we?" she asked him. "And they do want to come and see Bertie, don't they?"

"Yes, but we can't be on the tv, darling."

"Why not, Dad?"

"Because – because it wouldn't be fair on Bertie," he replied.

"Bertie wouldn't know he was on tv," Carrie argued. "Anyway, I thought you'd like it. I thought you'd like to be on That's Life with Bertie. It makes you laugh. It's the only thing that makes you laugh."

"I can't be on tv, Carrie. I'm not good enough to be on tv," her Dad said softly, sadly.

"Yes you are, love," Bridget said gently. "Yes, you are."

With great reluctance, Derek telephoned the number at the foot of the letter and the film crew from the BBC arrived at their home in Welwyn Garden City. It was a Saturday so there was no work for Dad in London and no school for Carrie. At first, Carrie was very upset that Esther hadn't come herself, but the film crew was very friendly and the man who was going to interview Dad was often on the TV with Esther and he explained that Esther was very busy and she had been so disappointed not to have been able to come herself, but would he do in her place because he really did like pigs?

Although it was morning, the day was already hot. Bertie was pleased to be under cover of the trees in the wood. He scurried from tree to favourite tree, churning up the grass and mud beneath with his snout.

"Bertie, Bertie, come here," one of the new men that had come on their walk today called to him. Bertie looked up and thought about the command for a second, before deciding that this new human wasn't as interesting as the oak tree roots that he was investigating.

"Bertie, Bertie, this way," Derek commanded and this time Bertie obediently trotted in the direction which he was called.

A patch of glorious yellow sunshine lit up the woodland floor in front of Bertie. Derek knew that the pig would not be able to resist. Bertie squealed in pure pleasure and launched himself into the pool of light, diving in, rolling around, scratching his back on the warm earth, and slowly relaxing his body until he lay quite still on his back with his legs stretched to the sky, a dozy, peaceful look on his face. The film crew caught it all on camera.

"Bertie, Bertie," Derek called. Bertie ignored him.

"Bertie, Bertie," Derek called again. "This way." Bertie continued to ignore him.

As discussed with the film crew, Derek made a great pantomime of looking at his watch and pretending to be bored of waiting for Bertie to finish dozing in the sun. Bertie ignored him.

"Come on Bertie," Derek said, and seeing as the pig was not going to budge, Derek got down onto all fours and crawled alongside him. Bertie continued to ignore him, He wriggled deeper into the earth and grass, scratching his back in a sensuously satisfying way.

"Come on, Bertie," Derek repeated, and then he began to grunt and squeal and make all kinds of strange noises. Bertie opened one eye to look at Derek.

Derek nuzzled Bertie and butted him gently with his forehead. Then he crawled a little along the path in the direction which they had been going before Bertie had been tempted by the beautiful golden pool.

The cameraman captured it all on film. The sound guy could hardly stop himself from laughing out loud and spoiling the recording. It was just so ridiculous, this smart London sales executive, who they had interviewed in serious mode in his home, now pretending to be a pig in the woods.

The director nodded to Carrie and as agreed she called,

"Bertie, Bertie come here."

Bertie stood up and obediently trotted after Carrie leaving Derek crouched on the woodland floor. Another walker in the woods passed by and looked at Derek incredulously, her dog, a little spaniel, bounded over to sniff the man on the ground. All the while Carrie, laughing, continued along the path followed by a happy pig and all the while the film crew was recording.

"Cut!" the director ordered. He was pleased with what was going to be excellent footage and would be a very funny item in next weekend's programme.

What the camera didn't see, and what maybe it should have done, was Derek wiping the tears of laughter from his eyes, getting up from all fours and running towards Carrie; swooping his little girl into his arms, and holding her tight. They laughed and laughed, until their stomachs ached and their sides cramped, while Bertie, their pig, gently butted their shins with his head.

19.

THE WOMAN WHO LOST HER VOICE (THE MUSES)

She had looked everywhere for it. Everywhere. At first, she had looked in the obvious places; her handbag, coat pockets, behind the sofa. Then she had looked in the less obvious; under her desk, at the end of the garden, in the fridge. But it was nowhere. The trouble was she couldn't retrace her steps to find it because she couldn't remember losing it. It made her question if she had ever had her voice at all.

"Of course you had a voice, darling – you never stopped prattling and dreaming when you were a child," Felicity's mother assured her.

For an instant, she was catapulted back in time to the plump little girl with big blue eyes and fair hair wearing a bright red and green cotton print sundress playing alongside the gaudy late summer dahlias. Queen of a make-believe world in a palace constructed by her dad under the pine tree at the end of their garden; a palace built from planks and poles with an old side gate that opened up and out for the roof. The palace was a sailing ship, a rocket, a school, a perfume factory. A magical place where she was a heroine, a hero, a villain, a scientist, a farmer, a princess.

"Yes," her older self agreed, she had had her voice when she was a child. But when had her voice vanished?

She must have had her voice at school. All teenagers have voices, don't they? Emerging adults brimming with ideas of what is right and good, just and of value; brains overflowing with creativity. Felicity felt that if she had had her voice in adolescence then it had probably been crushed by the weight of expectation loaded on her by exams, the chasing of each little mark on every single paper to place her firmly beyond the boundary of each grade.

Thinking about it, she couldn't remember having a voice at work. Getting up every day at 6.15 am. Hastily washing, skipping breakfast, and walking to the station to catch the 7.10 am train; mascara and eye-liner applied somewhere near Finsbury Park as experience showed that was where the tracks were the least bumpy so the results were less disastrous. Working briskly preparing reports, attending meetings, answering e-mails all day before returning shattered by 9 pm. There was no room for a voice in those years. So maybe it was her own fault that she had lost it, by letting herself become too busy? Or maybe she had lost her voice simply by growing up. Felicity sighed; she felt it was probably more complicated than that.

Well, if she couldn't find her voice and if she couldn't remember what had happened to it then she had better find a new one.

"I would start at the library if I were you," advised her mother sitting in her kitchen whilst Maggie, their mobile hairdresser nodded, in agreement as she applied her client's new colour.

The library had recently been refurbished and was a friendly welcoming place. Young parents, carers and grandparents chased toddlers across the entrance. Excited little people ran to the children's section at the back of the building where they could roll on cushions, dive into boxes of fairy-tales and picture books, be entertained by the lovely lady with the beautiful voice who read to them as they tried to sit attentively in a circle and who made them laugh when it was time for songs and rhymes. Students took their bags and laptops to the bright, quiet study space at the top of the stairs. Older members of the town, sat with the newspapers and magazines in the comfortable chairs by the entrance.

Armed with two volumes of history, an Atlas, and a bag of apples, she sat down in a bright alcove to read. As she read she became more and more excited. Six apples later she had learned that Ancient Greece was the birthplace of literary creativity because those lucky Greeks had nine Muses to help them. Obviously what she needed was a Muse of her very own. Easy, like getting a puppy for Christmas!

In a whirlwind of activity, she booked time off work, arranged her flights and hotel accommodation, and set off for Greece. She wasn't worried about being a young woman alone on holiday. She was on a mission, she was in Greece to get a Muse and nothing could deflect her from her intention. How picturesque the ruins were and how hot, Felicity thought, as she stood in the great Temple of Apollo at Delphi surrounded by tourists. Embarrassed, she delivered her request to the oracle under her breath for a Muse of her very own. She waited patiently for a clap of thunder or a bolt of lightning. Nothing! Instead, as she turned to leave in disappointment a very small lady in a museum attendant's uniform shuffled towards her and said in a thick Greek accent,

"Excuse me, Madame, do I understand you want a Muse?"

Felicity's surprised face conveyed her answer.

"Follow me," the museum attendant whispered huskily.

Filled with curiosity Felicity left her tour group unnoticed and followed the attendant until they reached an olive grove where nine beautiful ladies stood arranged in statuesque poses. Each had her hair tied up at the back of her head in an elegant knot. Each wore a floating tunic dress in a different pastel shade secured with a gold cord at the breasts and hips. The style flattered the figure and was Alma Tadema elegant. On their feet, each Muse wore simple brown leather sandals.

"Please Madame, be happy to meet the Muses of ancient Greece:

Calliope, Muse of Epic Poetry
Clio, Muse of History
Erato, Muse of Lyric Poetry
Euterpe, Muse of Music
Melpomene, Muse of Tragedy
Polyhymnia, Muse of Sacred Poetry
Terpsichore, Muse of Dance and Chorus
Urania, Muse of Astronomy, and,
Thalia, Muse of Idyllic Poetry!"

In the shadow of the grove, each lovely lady smiled serenely, nodding graciously as one by one they were introduced to the sweaty base-ball capped tourist.

Felicity was taken aback.

"All of them Muses?" she gasped.

"That's right Madame, which one would you like?" the museum attendant inquired.

Felicity wasn't sure. Each Muse had her merits and it would be cruel to separate them from each other.

"I'll take them all," she declared resolutely.

How she managed to get all the Muses back to the hotel she would never know. Squeezing everyone onto the minibus was a challenge. Erato knew some pretty good rhymes and after the stop at the vineyard, which had been programmed for the return journey, all the tourists and the Muses found the rhymes increasingly hilarious. Although Felicity wondered quietly to herself if Erato's rhymes were not quite in the classical taste.

No matter, that journey was nothing compared to the one back to England. Keeping the Muses under control at the airport was like shepherding cats. The Muses were in their element in the Duty-Free. Melpomene could hardly be persuaded away from the chocolate counter. Felicity shrugged, with that much tragedy in a girl's life chocolate was a deserved recompense. Thalia covered herself in makeup samples and Calliope stared longingly at the alcohol.

It did not take the Muses long to settle into life at Felicity's home in the apple tree town, although ten women sharing one bathroom was a little difficult before Polyhymnia devised a rota. Each Muse took inspiration from her new life in England, producing songs and poems of profound beauty. They still found time to complete the domestic chores that Felicity insisted that they share. Melpomene, Muse of Tragedy, produced some interesting baking whilst Euterpe, Muse of Music, took naturally to gardening where all the birds of the neighbourhood found her a fellow songster.

Felicity found that she had never had so many friends, as everybody she had ever met seemed to find a reason to pass by her house so that they could meet the Muses.

"It's so busy and so noisy, there's nothing but poetry, music, and drama from dawn to dusk. I can't even hear myself think, let alone hear myself read these poems that Erato's been helping me write," Felicity lamented to her mother one afternoon as her mother sat in her kitchen with her hair in a rather fetching Greek knot that Maggie had just completed under Thalia's guidance.

"Never mind, darling, the Muses are far better than those cheap little statues tourists normally bring home and you can't say this isn't fun,' her mother said eyeing Thalia's sandals and wondering at the same time if they were comfortable and came in her size.

"It's no use," Felicity moaned to her best friend Clare over a cappuccino two days later. "Just when I'm beginning to find my voice all the noise in my house is stifling it."

Clare commiserated, as sympathetically as a best friend could, looking so pretty with her hazelnut hair tied up with a ribbon in a Greek knot, pastel tunic dress, and sandals.

"You could always send them back," Clare suggested stirring the froth on her cappuccino and licking it off the spoon. "SAGA do great cruises – all you'd have to do is put the girls on a cruise in the direction of the Greek Islands and I'm sure they could manage on their own from there."

The girls objected vehemently to the proposal of an over 50s cruise when Felicity suggested it. Tears welled up in Euterpe's olive-green eyes.

"Felicity, how could you be so cruel to separate me from Damian?" she lamented. (She had recently begun dating the neighbour at the end of the garden).

"That is the last time I will provide you and your guests with honey cakes," Melpomene declared darkly as she stalked regally away into the kitchen.

Felicity could smell the offence she had caused.

"Oh dear," she sighed as she bought ten cream buns from the local bakery with the £20 prize money she had won in the *Look Now!* magazine short story competition that she had entered with a much better than she had thought little tale about lovers in a garden, inspired by Euterpe and Damian.

"Clare, please, you've really got to help me," she begged into her mobile phone as she sat in the town's central boulevard watching the fountain shoot graceful jets of ice-blue water into the air which shattered into thousands of raindrops in the circular pool at its base; the cream buns arranged neatly in a white cardboard box tied up with a mint green ribbon on the seat beside her.

"Well can you think of anywhere a bit Greek nearby?"

Felicity pulled a face. There wasn't anything Greek about Welwyn Garden City – except perhaps the Greek restaurant. Do you suppose the management needs nine waitresses with literary leanings?

Absent-mindedly she wound a loose lock of blondish hair, which had escaped from her Grecian knot, around a cherry red painted fingernail. Having the Muses to stay was a lot of fun and honestly, they'd been so helpful, not just with ironing but with her writing too. Living with nine creative souls had rubbed off on her and she had scribbled sonnets, devised dramas, and perfected poems with their help. What a shame she couldn't write her house bigger.

Clio cried next to the delicate pink roses growing a pattern on the whitewashed walls of the little house in the pocket-handkerchief garden. Glistening tears dripped down her alabaster cheeks and fell with a splash at her brown sandaled feet, miniature lakes for ants. Her sisters flourished in England but she, Clio Muse of History, was cut off from her roots; and to emphasise this melancholy thought she plucked a pale rosebud and fastened it to her breast to blossom, wither and die through the hot afternoon.

"Maybe a colour would lift your spirits, dearie – pink highlights would be very pretty. Maggie will be here any minute to do them if you like?" Felicity's mother suggested, wrapping the wan Muse in her maternal concern and concocting a plan.

The next morning Felicity's mother arrived at the little house with sandwiches, fruit, and bottles of water parcelled in eleven assorted satchels.

"A walk," she declared to Felicity and the nine.

"In the countryside," for clarification.

"It's a beautiful summer's day," for the reason.

"But the girls only have sandals," Felicity objected.

"So do I!" The retaliation. "For goodness sake Felicity, it's only 5 miles, 10 there and back." The final words.

The Muses gloried in the woodland, the lanes, the open fields. But you should have seen their faces when they spied the Palladian church at Ayot St Lawrence across the wildflower field; graceful Grecian columns bleached white, a Mediterranean temple under a Mediterranean sun. Their sandaled feet hardly touched the grass path as they flew to the Greek edifice in an English field. They draped themselves happily on the portico and pretended to be statues between the pillars.

"Thank you!" beamed Clio from the portico steps.

"You're welcome," Felicity replied. And after all, she thought to herself, five miles there and five miles back is an awful lot nearer than going to Greece. Then putting her writer's notebook aside she climbed up in between the columns and played with the Muses.

20.

DIGSWELL HOUSE

Marcus nosed his car carefully past the now fully grown shrubs at the entrance to Digswell House and parked on the gravel in front of the elegant cream building.

"This isn't the best view of it," he said apologetically to Heather who was sitting in the passenger seat alongside him. "It's much more impressive from the back lawn." He knew. He remembered.

Heather turned her head to kiss him, giving reassurance through her lips, before pressing the button to undo her seatbelt.

"It looks lovely," she said truthfully.

The estate agent had already arrived and was waiting by the steps up to the front door.

"Mr Simpson?" she greeted Marcus, extending her hand for a business-like shake "and Ms…?"

The agent was perplexed as to exactly who the woman accompanying her client was. He had booked the appointment online leaving skimpy personal details. Mr Simpson, she could see now, must easily be in his seventies; his hair, although still thick was white rather than grey, whereas the woman who accompanied him seemed the age of a daughter. She was slim with shoulder-length brown hair, slightly greying, which gave the effect of expensive highlights rather than of age. Yet she couldn't be his daughter, as she had just kissed him in the car, in the way lovers do. Her eyes flashed to Heather's hands where a large ruby ring decorated her left ring finger.

"This is Heather Godwin, my fiancée," Marcus introduced Heather.

Heather smiled directly and defiantly at the estate agent. She had seen the flick of her eyes to the ruby ring. Most people reacted in the same way, astonished that a woman of her age would be marrying a man the age of Marcus. But then they didn't know Marcus.

"Have you travelled far?" the estate agent asked quickly, trying to bring the conversation back to a place of sales.

"From Harrow," he replied.

Funny how you always feel you need to explain yourself further to estate agents Heather thought briefly to herself before augmenting his response,

"Marcus has recently retired and we want to be more in the country, but not too far from his kids."

"Where do they live?"

"Welwyn Garden City and Harpenden," Heather answered for Marcus who had his eyes fixed on the door.

Marcus let introductory chat float over him and away on the faint summer breeze. It was so different from the day he had first arrived here. That day was bitter and grey, a January horror when the sun hardly shows itself. He had walked with his suitcase and backpack from the station, not wanting to spend the little money he had in his wallet on a taxi. The walk up the hill from the town had been longer than he had thought it would be and he was soaked through. He had rung the bell and Dana had answered.

"So, you are retired, Mr Simpson?" the estate agent questioned.

"Yes, that's right."

"What did you do?" the estate agent asked, surreptitiously digging for the information on these people's finances and thus the potential of a sale.

"I was an artist. I mean, I am an artist. Until last year I illustrated books for a living, but now I am going to draw for pleasure."

"An artist – how interesting. Digswell House used to belong to the arts trust and artists used to live here."

Marcus nodded.

"And you, Ms Godwin? What do you do?"

"I'm a freelance editor."

"It's how we met," Marcus said proudly.

The estate agent smiled inwardly, their profile fitted the apartment well, she would work hard for this possible sale.

"You probably know the property dates from the early nineteenth century," the estate agent commenced her pitch. "It was built in the neoclassical style for the local aristocracy

– the Cowper family. They owned many estates in this area of Hertfordshire."

Heather caught Marcus's eye and twitched her nose playfully; verbs and adjectives in their secret language of looks and expressions. She could tell he wasn't listening to the estate agent.

"Very interesting!" Heather commented, so as not to appear rude. "What else do you know about the property?"

"During the first world war it was a hospital, as many of our large country houses were, but not for our soldiers – for the Australians. During the second world war it was a conference centre with many distinguished visitors, even Gandhi, and of course, George Bernard Shaw, who lived locally."

The estate agent was getting into her stride. The apartments in Digswell House were rather lovely, but it was the history of the house which was its primary selling point after its location.

"Shall we go through to the apartment?" she suggested. She opened the door with her key and lead Marcus and Heather through.

"After the war, the property was used as a boarding house for Sherrardswood school and in 1959 the house was taken over by the Digswell Arts Trust to provide accommodation and studio space for artists."

Dana had opened the door the day he had first arrived and the cold wind that buffeted the soaking Marcus now turned its attention with excitement to the dramatic figure on the threshold, picking upon the tresses of curls that had escaped from a knot, fixed absent-mindedly, at the back of her head.

"You'd better come in," she had said, and she had pulled him into the house, shutting the door firmly behind him.

"Grotty day isn't it?" she had remarked cheerfully. "You must be the new one they said was coming into the second-floor studio. I'm Dana. Would you like some tea? We've got beer if you prefer. What's your line? Painting I presume, most of the guys here paint. Don't suppose you have any weed do you? Gosh you are rather young aren't you?" Her words rushed out of her like marbles onto a tile floor, quick and well-formed and rolling in disparate directions.

He had been confused by her judgement of him; pleased he looked man enough to carry weed but disappointed he was so obviously a painter.

"Yes, I know," he said to the estate agent, "I lived here for not quite a year in the early '70s."

"Really?" Now it was the turn of the estate agent to be genuinely interested. "I've never had the opportunity to meet anyone who lived here in those years. What was it like? Was it as commune-like as I suppose?"

"Not really," Marcus lied. "We were very focused on our art."

The estate agent turned the key to the first-floor apartment.

"The trust gave up the house in the 1980s. That's when all these beautiful apartments were created and they've been refurbished extensively since." Then she added with a flirtatious little sales giggle, "Regency mansion flats are romantic but Regency washing facilities aren't!"

Heather and Marcus followed her to the front entrance of the apartment they had arranged to view. The dim hallway was hung with paintings of birds in a Georgian style. It led them to a light, bright sitting room. The carpet was cream with an expensive-looking rug next to the hearth, it was a sumptuous cacophony of blues; powder to duck-egg to peacock. A large gilt-edged mirror, hanging above the mantlepiece collected the light from the window and flung it aggressively back into the room. All the furniture was antique, except for a modern chrome reading-light hovering over one of the armchairs.

The room hadn't looked like this when Dana was in residence. Then it had been a tangled jumble of pots and half-finished clay birds. Piles of books made columns beside piles of her clean laundry. Her worn clothes were left to drape artistically over whatever item happened to be closest to hand when she took each garment off; stockings on chairbacks, scarves on the mantlepiece, jeans in the hearth. Cigarette buts over-flowed the ash-trays placed at convenient points around the room. The only patch of order was around her work table at the window, where she kept her tools in meticulous order.

He walked over to the window to touch the potter's table that was there but which he couldn't see.

"It's a lovely view of the garden isn't it?" the estate agent commented, thinking Marcus was drawn to what lay the other side of the glass, as most clients were. "It's a Capability Brown Landscape," she continued.

"Really?" Heather exclaimed. "How wonderful!"

Heather moved over to Marcus and linked her arm through his.

"It's lovely, isn't it?" she smiled and turned to look at him. "Was it always like this?"

Marcus looked out across the lawn and saw Dana walk towards him. In the moonlight, she had floated over the grass, ghost-like. Her white satin nightdress clung to her as if she had stepped out of water, showing every curve of her body. One spaghetti strap had slipped off her shoulder exposing her breast and nipple. He had watched her until she had slipped from his view into the house. Then he had lain in his bed and imagined his hands caressing the shape of her body as a sculptor caresses clay and stroked himself.

"Are you alright, darling?" Heather asked.

"Yes, I'm fine."

Heather inspected the rest of the rooms in the apartment. Marcus stayed looking out of the window, he knew what was in the apartment and what he would no longer find there.

"It's good, but you really ought to try working in clay," Dana had suggested, a cigarette trailing from the corner of her red painted lips, as she leant over his shoulder to look closely at his painting of a naked girl bathing in a glade. "You're never going to understand flesh and limbs until you feel form beneath your hands. You really are very young, aren't you?"

Dana could only give praise with one breath and take it away with the next. She might have been genuinely trying to help him improve but all she did was stress his inexperience. He watched her with the other artists; sometimes serious, sometimes flirtatious, sometimes with words full of kindness and occasionally burning with anger and contempt. She seemed to treat each member of the artistic community completely differently from one day to the next. He followed her around the house like a puppy, hanging off her every word, every glance.

She took him to her studio where she handed him clay. They sat side by side at her table each working their hands through an identically sized lump. She showed him how to press the clay into the shape of a pot, to squeeze the lip with his fingertips, to rub and to roll the clay in his palms. She praised his effort and then laughed at his attempt.

"That is such a schoolboy pot," she declared in honesty. And then she led him by the hand to the bedroom where she showed him how to press and squeeze, to rub and to roll – praising him and laughing at him in equal measure.

"Not such a schoolboy now," she said acidly under the sheets before stroking his chest tenderly. "Not such a schoolboy now," as she drew him into her.

"Were any of the artists you knew while you were here famous?" the estate agent asked. She had abandoned the sale. Anyone who only looked out of the window and didn't view all the rooms was never going to make a purchase, but the old man still might be good for some information.

"No, not really," Marcus answered. "Not unless you count Dana Willis."

"Dana Willis? Who was she?"

"She was a very talented ceramist. Ironically she didn't sell much of her work in the UK, it was more sought after in the States. She left Digswell a little before I did and moved to New York. She did quite well out there, but she died in the mid-eighties. Lots of artists did you know."

The estate agent didn't know. She was too young to remember.

He had loved Dana Willis passionately, besottedly. There was no point to Digswell House without her, and he left shortly after she did.

"It's all very lovely," Heather said in a tone to end the viewing. "Marcus and I will have a chat and we'll let you know. Is it alright if we take a walk on the back lawn before we go? It will only be for a few minutes as we have another appointment."

The estate agent left them, she too had another appointment, which might be more lucrative than this one had been. She knew where Marcus and Heather would be heading next; to Marden Hill at Tewin, where a similar apartment was on the market for a similar price with a similar agent. It would suit them better. She silently wished them well and then forgot all about them, remembering only to look up the artist Dana Willis in case knowledge of the woman might be useful to sell this flat.

Heather took Marcus's hand in hers and they walked onto the back lawn. The rear of the house was, as Marcus had said, much more impressive, with four Greek columns and a peaceful tree-lined view across the Mimram valley.

"Are you pleased you came back to see the house?" Heather asked.

"Yes, I am," he replied, "I couldn't pass up a viewing, knowing it was on the market."

Heather reached up to kiss him. She wasn't threatened by the living love of a dead woman, nor the dead love of a living woman.

"I think Marden Hill will suit us better," she said simply.

He put his arm around his fiancée and turned back to look at the elegant house.

"It's funny how a building can go through as many changes and identities over the years as a person can," he commented.

"True," Heather reflected. "But it can never go back to what it was before. It will always be different. Come on darling, let's go to Marden Hill, I'll drive."

And she drove him away from a place he couldn't go back to; to a place where together they could go forward.

21.

THE BIRTHDAY

Birthdays. Ada smiled gently to herself as she sat in the place of honour on a very long table, which seemed to take up the entirety of the Italian restaurant. Funny how you can remember every birthday as a child and yet as an adult how frequently you forget your age and have to deduct the year you were born from the year it is now to arrive at a number that seems incredible and not worth remembering. She knew how old she was today though. Today was a special birthday and one that the family had been planning for months. She wasn't sure exactly which one of the family had been responsible for the organisation, probably Michael, more likely Louisa. She was grateful for the effort and had been looking forward to today for weeks.

Ada shifted her weight in her wheelchair.

"Are you comfortable, Granny?"

Michael, her clever engineer grandson, by her side, was swift to notice and move closer to help her alter her position. She smiled lovingly at him and reached to take his hand, hoping that her mouth didn't look as gruesome as it felt over her false teeth. They were such an uncomfortable nuisance.

"We are so lucky that the dentist managed to rush through a new set of teeth for Mum for today," Ada heard her daughter Anne tell a young student further along the table. Now, who was that pretty girl? Ada knitted her eyebrows together. She was sure someone had told her –

Anna, Annabel, Anna...lee, Anna something. Ada couldn't remember. Pretty girl though. Ada smiled and nodded at her.

"Mum keeps taking her teeth out and leaving them in tissues on her bedside table and the care home staff throw them out by mistake, we've lost 3 sets already!"

Ada heard a giggle from the young lady who could be Annabel. Yes, Annabel! Annabel, the girlfriend of Michael and Louisa's youngest, Leigh. They were both studying physics at Birmingham. She remembered it now, it just took her a bit of time. She smiled triumphantly at Annabel and Leigh. Perhaps there would be a wedding. Ada liked weddings. Michael's wedding had been beautiful and they had eaten apple crumble. Anyway, what do you need teeth for? You don't need teeth to eat pudding.

She had chosen spaghetti bolognese from the menu. It was the only name of a dish she recognised. She quite liked the spiral pasta she sometimes ate at the care home but goodness knows what it was called. Bolognese was fine.

"I like bolognese too," announced six-year-old Jake sitting next to his mother Tamsin and granny Anne. The two ladies rolled their eyes at each other in anticipation of the mess that could be made by the youngest and the oldest at the party.

"Well I like ice cream," Ada said emphatically.

"The birthday girl can most definitely have ice cream," laughed Michael as the spaghetti was placed in front of her.

"Let me cut the spaghetti up for you, Granny," Andrew offered.

Andrew was sitting on her other side; such a handsome man, so like how his father looked at his age. His father, her lovely boy Roger. Whereas Michael, Andrew's brother, could be the carbon copy of their grandfather, her beloved husband Lawrence. For an instant, a shadow passed over Ada's face. Not everyone from her precious family was present and never could be. It was so cruel that two men so beloved could pass away before her.

"Mummy, can I give Granniest her present now?" Ada heard a little voice pipe, as Tamsin's daughter, Charlotte, crept in beside her in the space next to Andrew. She looked so sweet, so little, Ada reached out her hand to stroke the child's cheek. A bony, shrivelled hand that looked like it would fall to pieces under the pressure of an overzealous touch, but a hand that still had strength, that still had personality.

"Thank you, sweetheart."

Ada tore at the pretty floral paper like a three-year-old and found beneath a box labelled 'luxury photo-frame.' She looked up with thanks and smiled proudly round at her family along the length of the table, chatting, laughing, pleased to be with each other, young cousins playing, nieces and nephews catching up. Which one of them would have arranged a family photograph for her? Probably Michael, no most likely Louisa. They all knew how much she loved photos. Her little room in the care home was a veritable portrait gallery of images in sepia, black and white and colour

– all sizes, family groups, school uniforms, graduation, holiday snaps, new babies, weddings. Photographs that scanned the decades of her life, more even, as in her gallery were Victorian portraits of her long passed-away parents as children and an especially precious war-time wedding snap, her father in uniform for King and Country. Some days she spent hours in her wheelchair just looking at her family gallery, remembering and reliving.

"Shall I open it, Granniest?" Charlotte asked impatiently. Ada loved the name her great-granddaughter had invented. Charlotte was too young in years to understand the concept of generations but she did understand 'most' and this old lady with unstable teeth – there one day and gone the next – who was her Mummy's Granny, owned more years than anyone else she knew.

"Yes please, darling," Ada croaked in the old lady's voice she still found hard to recognise.

Out from the box appeared a gleaming silver photograph frame. Charlotte placed it carefully in Ada's arthritic hands and Ada held it in her lap, silently and gazed at the photo. It was a wide landscape with a summer green field in the foreground looking down on and over a town nestled between trees. Drawing her eyes to the town, inviting her to leave her viewpoint on the hill were the elegant arches of the Digswell viaduct straddling the valley. Ada touched the viaduct with her finger, tracing its line from the edge of the photo to the point where it disappeared, dissolving amongst trees and town. She might not be able to walk but she could still see detail and she could still remember. She moved her forefinger away from the viaduct and the railway line it carried. Now she traced the shape of her beloved home town, finding the landmarks with her fingertip until it arrived at the unmistakable white silos of the iconic Shredded Wheat factory.

Birthdays. Ada gazed at the photo.

Of all the birthdays she could remember, that day had been the most special. It had been a Sunday. Her weeks were long and monotonous at the silk stocking factory, Fedden and Bond, but the Barclay corset factory was soon to open and she intended to apply for a promoted position. Saturday evenings were for dancing but Sundays were heavenly, a whole day with Lawrence, walking in the countryside that cradled their young town. Lawrence had a good job at the Wheat factory. At twenty-three years old he floated through life with a charming manner and an inclination to work hard. His aptitude had been noted and he was working his way up the factory ranks.

Her parents, joyous that her father had survived the horrors of Flanders, had moved out from East London in 1920. Her father, Jim, was a small man, but he had the strength of an ox, physically and mentally. He wanted more for his family than the East End could give. He wanted to obliterate the war in a place of opportunity in a town which met the countryside. And so, unafraid of being pioneers, he and his wife Nancy were among the first to arrive at the new town. Ada, already growing in her mother's womb when she had arrived, had known no other home than the white-fronted semi-detached cottage with its little front garden and delightful back lawn. Lawrence's family had arrived in 1933 but, strangely, their paths didn't cross in that small town until two years later, at a dance at The Cherry Tree, she a mere seventeen and he an exciting twenty-one. They returned regularly to dance until all their friends and respective families were hopefully certain the two were a couple.

They were well suited; they both appreciated the opportunities that they had and neither worried unduly about the approaching political storm. Both came alive with physical activity – dancing at The Cherry Tree or walking in the countryside.

On that special, sunny, happy Birthday, Lawrence held her hand as they made their way up the hill away from the viaduct to their favourite spot on the heights overlooking the town. In his other hand, he held a hamper and he carried a backpack on his shoulders.

"Here we are Ada, my dear," he pronounced, halting their progress and turning round to survey the view. Behind them further up the hill, a tight copse of trees, a boundary between the farmer's fields and the ancient village at the summit. In front of them, their new town snuggled into the natural dip of the scooped valley. The chalky white silos of the Shredded Wheat factory reflected the light like a beacon. Further away on the horizon stood London. Ada thought it was incredible that such a large city could be so close and so hidden among the trees and the fields of the intervening landscape.

Lawrence produced a red tartan blanket from his backpack. He laid it on the ground, assiduously smoothing out all the creases, and pressing down the grasses beneath it until it was perfectly flat.

"Your Highness," he motioned to her to sit with a bow.

"Don't be silly, Lawrence," Ada giggled.

"Today is your birthday and you shall be treated like a princess."

So she sat, ankles together, skirt drawn down over her knees, and allowed him to give her the birthday he'd so carefully planned.

"It's so lovely here," she sighed as she looked out from the heights across the new town and up to the handsome face of her beau.

"Yes it is, Ada, a special place,' he agreed.

He opened up the hamper.

"First plates and cutlery for her Highness, then, ah yes, ducks breast and – apples!" he chuckled at the curious lunch combination.

As dapper as a waiter at a high-class London restaurant, Lawrence served the birthday picnic lunch for them to share. It was delicious.

"And now, the pièce de resistance – cake!" Lawrence declared.

With the utmost care, he lifted a light cardboard box from the hamper and placed it gingerly on the blanket in front of Ada. Birthday cake, it had to be birthday cake. Ada, who loved all things sweet, rushed to open the flaps of the box, not at all carefully or gingerly. Inside were two large slices of Victoria Sponge, dripping with raspberry jam and covered with confectioner's sugar, and nestled between the slices was a small navy box.

She was stopped dead in her tracks of intention. Confusion covered her. Could it be what she thought?

"Lawrence," she whispered, seeking confirmation in his brown eyes.

"Go on," he urged quietly.

She picked up the box, hardly daring to believe it contained what she thought. There inside was the most exquisite, darling gold band, set with a diamond solitaire.

Ada's face lit up with the most beautiful smile that Lawrence could have ever imagined. A more perfect 'yes' than any syllable could possibly convey.

How many birthdays had she spent subsequently at that same spot? How many times had she returned with children and grandchildren and alone?

She felt her daughter Anne come close to her on the other side of little Charlotte. Anne put her arms around her mother in a warm hug.

"You always loved the heights so much Mum, we used to go there all the time with Roger and Daddy. I couldn't get you to the heights, with your wheelchair, but I could get the heights to you. Happy Birthday!"

Ada held her daughter tight, one old lady and one very old lady, remembering.

22.
OLIVIA'S APPLE TREE

Olivia lay under the old apple tree looking up at the pink and white blossom bobbing in the breeze against the blue spring sky. Bees from the hive at the end of the garden called busily from blossom cluster to blossom cluster, collecting packages of waxy golden nectar on their spindly legs and dustings of pollen specks on their yellow and black bodies. The tree was so beautiful. She wished it would stay dressed in pink forever. She imagined climbing up the tree to gather armfuls of petals to assemble into a white Cinderella dress with pink-tinted flounces fit for a fairy ball. Or even better, maybe she would spend the night under the stars in the boughs of the tree, nestling into the blossom clusters in the same way as each night she snuggled under her unicorn patterned duvet. She wouldn't be cold, she'd wear a jumper of course! She knew she was old enough to know, now that she was eight, that every moment the blossom was out must be enjoyed before it fell from the tree to form a disappointing dirty brown carpet on the ground. But she also knew she was old enough to know that the short-lived blossom would bring delicious apples in the autumn, a whole different season to be enjoyed, and even better a season with a birthday, when she would be a whole year older.

She stretched out her arms and legs diagonally to make a five-point star, stretching to the tips of the fingers and the tips of her toes and through her neck to the crown of her head and beyond, feeling herself grow like the daffodils around her and the grass beneath her.

She heard steps approach and knew exactly who it was.

"What are you doing, Munchkin?"

She looked up to see her grandfather standing beside her looking down, a broad smile on his face.

"I'm growing under the apple tree, Grandfather."

"That sounds good. Can I join you?"

And getting down first on one knee and then on the other he rolled onto his back to lie next to his granddaughter. They both looked up, in five-point star shapes, at the tree above.

A moment passed.

"No, I don't think I'm growing, Olivia. Are you?"

"Yes, Grandfather. I'm definitely bigger than this morning."

He chuckled at her response,

"You are growing every day, Munchkin, but I am only shrinking. Why are we star shapes, Olivia?"

"Because that's the shape inside an apple."

"Of course, I should have known!" the not-too-old grandfather said, again with his trademark chuckle as he pushed himself up with his elbow. "And I bet you're hungry for an apple too," he continued, as he produced a golden ball flecked with scarlet from his trouser pocket and a penknife from the other. He cut Olivia's apple in half horizontally so that two perfect five-point stars were formed from the apple's core.

The pair bit with a crunch into their shared apple.

"This is the last apple left from the autumn from this tree," he said through a mouthful of fruit. "Do you remember how after we picked the apples we wrapped them in newspaper and packed them…"

"…in a box at the back of the shed," she interrupted through her mouthful of apple.

A pause.

"Grandfather?"

"Yes, Munchkin."

"Do apple trees die?"

"Yes, they do, Munchkin."

Another pause, half-eaten half apple hovering in the air midway between her lap and her mouth.

"When will our tree die, Grandfather?"

"It's a very old tree, Olivia. Apple trees only live for about a hundred years."

Her grandfather looked frankly into her enquiring eyes, knowing what question was likely to come next, wondering if he should give her space to let her ask, or stride into the vacuum and give her an answer to the question not yet fully verbalised or understood.

Max looked over her shoulder as she sat typing on her laptop at the dining room table, where he had placed a glass of water down for her to drink as she worked. He could never understand why she persisted in using such outdated technology. It caused no end of grief when she wanted to transfer files so that other people could use or read them.

"Look, I want to do it this way, I know it's old fashioned, I don't care," she had grumbled at him.

It was probably the way people used to think about writing by hand on paper. No one ever did that anymore. It was funny though because with her job she was completely tech-savvy – and was highly successful in her field – it was just at home on the dining room table for her writing it had to be a half-dead laptop.

"Do you mind?" he asked as he looked over her shoulder to peer at the screen.

"It's good," he encouraged. "What happened next?"

Olivia reached for the glass of water and took slow sips, finding it easier to place her lips on the cold glass than to use her lips to form words.

Max understood her silence, and so changed the direction of the conversation to a place where he knew she could find words.

"You know, I still find it amazing you can remember apple trees and bees," he said. "I mean, it's not like there's a huge age gap between us – only two years."

Olivia put down her glass.

"I guess that's enough to have made the difference," she replied. "You lay down a lot of memories between 6 and 8. Or maybe it's just you understand stuff more in those years?"

She looked at the screen: *Olivia's Apple Tree* she felt a huge swell of sadness roll achingly over her body and start tingling around her eyelashes.

"It's so hard, Max."

"I know, sweetheart." He hugged her. "What happened next?"

Olivia began typing again on the elderly keyboard, slowly at first and then picking up speed.

Her grandfather decided to step carefully into the child's unusual silence. There would be time enough to answer questions on his mortality.

"Do you know when this town was built, Munchkin?" he asked.

"Of course, Grandfather! Over one hundred years ago. We've learnt all about it at school. Didn't you know?" She was rather astonished that he might not know. But it was possible because at eight years old, she had worked out that adults didn't know everything.

"That's right, more than one hundred years ago in 1920. And it's a very special town..."

"Because every house has a garden and all the streets have grass and flowers, that's what makes it a Garden City," she informed him.

"And every garden had an apple tree."

"Every garden?"

"Yes, everyone coming to live in the new town had a new baby apple tree, to care for and to enjoy the delicious apples."

He waited for her to put the two pieces of information together. It wasn't long.

"Grandfather, that means this tree must be over one hundred years old."

"Yes, Munchkin."

"And it might die soon!"

"That's right, darling. Everything dies. But life goes on. Shall we plant a new baby tree so there will be a tree here in the garden ready to give us our apples when this old tree has died?"

"From the pips?" she asked excitedly looking at the remnants of the half core that she was twizzling between her third finger and her thumb as she spoke.

"Yes!"

She looked eagerly around, mentally planting the apple's pips in the four corners of the garden in spaces free from her grandfather's fruit trees and grandmother's roses.

Together they found a good spot in the hundred-year-old garden and planted the pips, Grandfather wondering to himself if the pips would germinate or whether they would end up at the garden centre choosing a new sapling.

Max was right. She could remember. She could remember the taste of apples, the crunch they made, apple juice chilled and refreshing from the fridge. And not just the apple trees, she could remember walking with her grandfather in the flower meadows at the edge of the wood and alongside the cornfields. She could remember fields – fields of corn, with poppies dotted amid the grass and daisies too. She could remember the bees, she could remember honey. It all changed. The pips never germinated and a sapling could not be bought.

It was hard for everyone to realise how it happened. The Crisis crept up on the world rather than exploding into it. All eyes were off the ball, focusing on the global health pandemic, which was of course terrible, but nothing compared to the environmental catastrophe that was to come. Although she had lived through what was now called 'The Crisis' she had only been a child and so couldn't fully appreciate it. She'd learnt about it properly at university.

It was all to do with the bees. Scientists and Conservationists had been calling for years for governments to take action. Bees were crucial to pollinating crops. But so much had been against them: global warming, pesticides, loss of habitat. Colonies and hives were already depleted before the early 2020s when an extraordinary harsh spring in the northern hemisphere combined with a global pandemic of the devasting varroa mite destroyed 90% of the world's bee population. She had studied it and had become an expert at it at university. At university, where she had also learnt about her Grandfather.

"Do you know who built our Garden City?" her Grandfather asked as they planted the pips.

"Ebenezer Howard!" But, Grandfather, you do know he didn't do it by himself, don't you? It was a big job to plan a new town, other people had to help him."

"Yes, of course, Munchkin, it always takes people working together to make things happen. Look at us working together to plant the baby tree."

Time for a lesson.

"Ebenezer Howard was a man of vision," he began.

"That's why he's looking into the distance."

Her grandfather was momentarily thrown from the lesson track,

"..distance?"

"Yes, the statue of Ebenezer Howard in the town centre is looking into the distance – Ebenezer's thinking about his new town – where everyone was going to get their own garden, and their own apple tree." Olivia felt proud of herself for having listened hard at school in lessons about her town's history.

Her grandfather smiled and reached down to smooth her hair which was tangled where she slept on it. She had run out forgetting to brush it that morning and now bits of grass, from where she had been lying, were added to the growing bird's nest on her head.

"Ebenezer Howard was a man of vision who wanted to make life better for the people that lived here and he believed that to make it better, town and countryside had to join together. People need both. We need our countryside, Olivia. We need our gardens with our apple trees and our bees," he explained as he walked over to the garden tap at the back of the house, where he filled the watering can standing next to it.

"And we need to look after them," he taught her, handing her the watering can to water the planted pips.

The sudden loss of the bees had launched a domino effect of tragedy; crops failed, famine struck, scientists scrambled to find new ways of feeding populations, riots broke out. Olivia remembered YouTube videos of armies of fruit workers spreading pollen manually from flower to flower in the orchards so that at least there would be some apples, peaches, plums. Prices rocketed, strawberries were virtually unheard of for more than a decade. Even now, more than twenty-five years later, orchards were only beginning to be re-established. It was hoped that soon the government would be able to stop adding vitamins to the water supply as the population would be able to get enough nourishment from fruit and vegetables.

Max had drawn a chair up next to Olivia as she typed. She didn't seem to mind.

"You know, it wasn't until I was at uni that I learnt who he really was," she said softly, still looking at the keyboard. She stopped typing and turned to look at her partner.

"He was so proud of me getting onto that course. I guess at A level you focus on facts not on who had discovered the facts or written about the facts and then suddenly at university every other paper or report had his name on. I couldn't believe that Grandfather was so... so important. He was just Grandfather, who liked to grow fruit trees and keep bees. How could I have known he was one of the country's experts?"

"I think it's hard for any child to understand what our parents work at, and even harder to imagine our grandparents' working lives. I mean, we only normally meet our grandparents when they have already retired," Max replied thoughtfully.

She wasn't listening. She was absorbed in her life story.

"He was so busy after The Crisis. He was always going off to meetings but I didn't realise. I just knew how upset he was about the bees. And there were so many problems everywhere — all because there were no bees. But there he was, all the time being a real Ebenezer."

"Now I'm lost, Olivia, 'a real Ebenezer'?"

She started to laugh. He was pleased.

"I remember when I was a little girl that Grandfather explained that the man who founded towns was called Ebenezer Howard and he was a man of vision. So was Grandfather. I learnt at uni that he came out of retirement and that he was the expert behind the government's strategy on how to revive the bee population from the tiny per cent that was left and how to manage our landscape to bring back the wildflowers. He was the man of vision. He knew that it was never too late to care for nature and to trust it."

"And now you are continuing it, Olivia, with your work at the Institute."

"Yeah," she nodded sadly, "right up until the end he liked to talk about it with me. It was great he never lost his memory."

There was no stopping the tears now. They swelled out of her eyes and would have wetted her lap but for the fact that Max was already holding her in his arms.

"Thank you," she sniffed.

"How will your eulogy story end?" he asked as he stroked the patch of hair on the back of her head that was always prone to tangles.

Olivia thought for a moment and turned back to her laptop. She said out loud as she typed,

And so Grandfather taught me that day in the garden what he had learned from a man who had lived one hundred years earlier; that everyone needs an 'apple tree in their garden' – everyone needs the opportunity to connect with nature and everyone has the responsibility to care for it. Thank you, Grandfather. I will never forget you."

PART 4: THE CITY
ST ALBANS

23.
PROSERPINA'S PROMISE

Paulina Marcia is playing on the mosaic floor not far from her mother's feet. She has a box, a wooden box, the size of a man's foot. Scattered over the mosaic patterns, next to the box, are ten wooden bricks stain-painted in red, green, ochre, even the blue of the heavens. The toy must have been expensive but her grandfather will spare no expense, not even for a granddaughter. Paulina has a concentration that astonishes her father and her grandfather, who cannot understand how a female child, and such a young one at that, can play the same game again and again without wearying. Julia understands. Julia understands patience and perseverance. She watches her little daughter pick each brick up and, with deep earnestness, place it in the box. She laughs with Paulina when all the bricks have found their home. She claps her hands in delight crying, "Well done my sweet one!" and bends forward, ignoring the discomfort, to kiss the child at her feet. Then Paulina tips the box over, sending the bricks clattering across the hard patterned floor, as much pleasure in the undoing, in the unravelling, in the destruction, as in the putting together. Julia settles back into her chair to watch Paulina start all over again, picking up each painted wooden brick and placing it in the box.

"Come, Paulina," Julia says, herself wearing of the game. "Shall I tell you a story?" She taps her lap, inviting her precious love to climb up for imagination and cuddles. But there is less space than there was before on that lap, that safe haven. Paulina is already aware of the unseen intruder.

"Me hung-ee mama," the little girl says instead and Julia rings the bell on the table beside her for the servant.

"Take Paulina to the kitchen for some of the stewed apples I asked you to prepare earlier," Julia commands. Paulina responds with a large smile and toddles away, her chubby fist holding the servant girl's hand. The toddling child lightly brushes the wall by the hearth, with her fingers of her un-held hand, before leaving the room.

Later, Julia sits close to the wall, next to the hearth, where the servant has made a fire to warm her mistress from the chill of the late November evening. Julia feels like an apple, ripe and smooth. Her skin, luscious and gleaming but thin, is stretched tight over her juicy female flesh; the seed inside, her baby. Her abdomen is hard like an apple. All the softness of her maiden body and early pregnancy is gone. She is ripe. Soon the apple will fall from the tree, soon her baby will birth from her body. She reaches, unconsciously, to the wall beside her and touches it gently with her fingers. She presses her weight into the tips, pushing power into the wall and then, relaxing her strength, pulls the power back into her hands as if bricks are a placenta. The pressure of her fingertips, a heartbeat.

Paulina is in her little bed asleep. Julia herself bathed her and brushed her baby's downy black curls, growing longer month by month. She dressed her child for the night herself and took Paulina by the hand to the altar to pray to the goddess. Her parents-in-law, in whose house she lives, turn a kindly blind eye to their daughter-in-law taking the role of a servant in the care of their granddaughter. Yet Paulinus their son, Julia's husband, joins her more than a man is expected in the rearing of his child. He stands at his wife's side to kiss the precious babe goodnight. Recently, he has started to sing to his daughter to sleep in his rich baritone voice, a silly little rhyme that delights the child now that she understands words. It lifts Julia's heart as she watches and listens. When he finishes his nonsense-lullaby and kisses the sleepy, raven-curled brow, he pulls Julia close to him, pulling her into his body. He places a hand on her belly, as if the strength in his embrace, in the palm of his hand, in his will, is enough to keep all of Julia safe.

From her chair next to the hearth and next to the wall, Julia can see the household shrine where the beautiful bronze Proserpina keeps watch over the family. The goddess is placed between two columns in the niche created especially for her. She is dancing across a pasture of golden buttercups and is only pausing briefly before dancing across the next. Her hair is flowing over her shoulders. Her loose skirts, billowing in the breeze and in the dance, are tied around her thighs. Her torso and breasts are bare. She holds an apple. The goddess' stomach is flat and maidenly, but Julia thinks, as she massages her baby hardness and acknowledges the slow tight movement in response beneath her skin, how easy it would be for the statue of the goddess to have been fashioned with a swollen belly like her own, the shape would fit perfectly into the space created by the loose skirts and would look just as beautiful, more so.

In the first months after her wedding, she had prayed half-heartedly to Proserpina to be fruitful. She knew not to expect a child immediately, her mother had warned her of that and so there seemed little point in spending too much time praying for something which would happen within the year. But months had passed, she had turned from 17 to 18, to 19 and still she had not been blessed with fruitfulness. Julia began to pray to the goddess in earnest. Paulinus was patient with her at first, but she could sense that his gentleness was ebbing, that his eye was roving. When she went with him to the theatre she dressed in her most flattering shades, she wore the combs in her hair he had given her for her wedding, she held onto his arm tight, to remind him she was with him, to remind him that she was his wife, and not to stray.

Her parents-in-law too were anxious. Julia had many brothers and sisters. Her parents were fruitful. Her father Julius was blessed in business. Already Julia was an aunt many times over. The omens for their son's marriage to Julia had been positive, the entrails of the lamb sacrificed at the temple had foretold blessing. What could be wrong with Julia that she had not given them a grandchild? Her mother-in-law, Livilla, visited the temple at each full moon and offered sacrifices for a grandson.

Julia persevered, now praying to Proserpina night and day. Proserpina, the dancing goddess of Springtime who had spent six months underground, a prisoner of Hades, in the dark, away from her mother Ceres, away from the sunshine and the joy of the world. She prayed that her own time of barrenness would end. There were days that she felt as if it were her, not Proserpina trapped in darkness, out of favour, alone, desperate. A prisoner of expectation in a body that was cursed. Yet the goddess continued to dance brightly towards her, from out of her alcove at the family shrine, across the field of golden buttercups, joy on her beautiful face. Spring would come for Julia too. She persevered, she waited and finally, she was rewarded.

Julia feels cold this evening, despite the fire, and rings the bell for her servant to bring her a shawl. The young girl helps her mistress place the warm woven fabric around her shoulders. Now that she is standing, Julia realises she feels more comfortable. She moves silently close to the wall, its red-painted decoration warm and inviting. She places her fingertips against the paint and kisses the wall softly and tenderly as she has many times before.

When she had told him that he was, at last, to be a father, Paulinus was surely the happiest man in the whole of Verulamium. He held his head up high as he walked the streets and there was a lightness of expectancy in his step, a bright future of dynasty was growing in his wife's womb. Her mother Marcia, her mother-in-law Livilla, her sisters, all gathered around her, no longer at a loss for words for Julia's barren condition, instead, full of encouragement and advice, as she had crossed the threshold of conception and was shortly to join them in the society of motherhood.

As her lips brush the warm red wall she feels her belly tighten, it catches her by surprise. A pain encircles her pelvis stretching round to her buttocks and her lower back. Involuntarily, she takes a sharp intake of breath and waits.

The pain passes. She moves closer to the wall and rests her forehead against it as if the wall can protect her from what is to come. She knows what the next hours will bring. This is the third time, she knows the pain and fear she has to face. Despite the happiness of the second, she always, and forever will be, hostage to the memory of the first.

Too long. It is taking too long. It is as if the body, which has not birthed before, does not know what to do. The midwife is tight-lipped. Julia strains and heaves with each wave of pain which engulfs her body in such quick succession she has no time to recover from the last. The herbs and the oils to cajole and persuade the baby into the world are long abandoned in bowls and jars around the room. Too long. It is taking too long. The midwife frets silently; she has attended too many births to miss the signs of the life which will not now come. Yet the struggle to bring to an end what has begun continues. Finally, the new life, which is not, is expelled from Julia's body. The midwife carefully wipes the tiny infant and wraps it in a square of fresh white linen. Julia's mother and mother-in-law gently raise her from the birthing stool to the bed, where she lies, exhausted, eyes-closed, hovering between worlds.

The midwife carefully passes the tiny bundle to Julia's mother-in-law, who opens the swaddling and examines the perfect baby, perfect in every way except in breath. A girl. She turns to Julia's mother who is stroking her daughter's brow and gripping her daughter's hand, urging Julia to turn around from the path she is on, to turn back to them, to come back to the Springtime, to resist the pull towards Hades and the darkness. The midwife is silently attending to the afterbirth.

Such sadness, such disappointment weighs heavy on Livilla as she holds the stillborn child and momentarily wonders what she should do. There is the father and the grandfather to be told. There are purification ceremonies that must be held. Instinctively, her hands and arms respond of their own accord and draw the baby close to her breast, as they have done countless times before when she was a young mother herself. She knows now what she should do. She moves to the bed, where Julia is lying robbed of colour as if already made of stone; where her mother, softly weeping, strokes her daughter's brow again and again.

"Julia," the mother-in-law says softly. There is no response from the bed.

"Julia, open your eyes, Julia!" Livilla now commands. "Here is your daughter; Paulina Livilla." Tenderly she places Julia's firstborn in her arms.

Julia feels the small weight and her eyes flutter open. Caught on the thresholds between the worlds, she stares hazily at the tiny treasure wrapped in white linen which lies in her arms. Paulina Livilla. Her daughter. Part of her forever. Will she follow the child, who had no life other than in her womb to Hades, or will she stay with her dead child's bones in Verulamium? The greyness which entombs her is too thick for her to tell. Her skin is too grey for Livilla and Marcia to tell. The blood is too red for the midwife to tell.

Julia lingers on the threshold until the goddess decides. Proserpina dances to Julia across the buttercups and kisses the young mother with sisterly tenderness. Spring will return. It always does.

The midwife is paid, the chamber cleaned, sacrifices made. Julia watches as part of herself, wrapped in pure white linen, is placed in a terracotta tile-lined cavity created in the wall next to the hearth. Her husband and her mother-in-law bless their namesake as the cavity is closed by the mason. Paulinus turns to his wife. She gives herself into his arms where, with grief breaking both their hearts, he holds her tight and safe. She will always live in this house, she could never live elsewhere. Part of herself will always be in this house. Over Paulinus' shoulder, she can see dancing, bright, Proserpina and her sadness starts to melt like the winter snow in the pale spring warmth. There will never be another Paulina Livilla, there will never be another spring the same as the one before. But there will be more. Proserpina has promised.

24.
BLEAK HOUSE

"Good morning, Mr Doyle," Nancy said nervously to her employer as she entered the breakfast room at the back of the house carrying a tray of toast and jam and a pot of piping hot coffee.

Mr Doyle caught the anxious edge to her voice and raised his eyes from the newspaper which he was perusing, rather than reading, to look at the young maid.

"Is all well, Nancy?" he enquired.

She placed the tray down in front of Mr Doyle and before transferring its burden to the table she took a deep breath and said in a rush, as if speed would mitigate the bad news,

"Mr Doyle, sir, Mrs O'Sullivan told me to tell you that there's another one of those women on the drive. She's doing her best to deal with her by herself but she might need some help."

"Not again!" Mr Doyle moaned. "This is the limit! How many times this month, Nancy?"

"At least a dozen, sir."

"And three this week I should think."

"It's the weather, sir," Nancy ventured to suggest.

Mr Doyle knitted his dark eyebrows together and furrowed his brow in an attempt to understand his maid,

"The weather?"

"Yes sir, now it's spring sir, the better weather makes them more adventurous and when there's little chance of rain they bring their sketch books."

"Sketch books!" he barked. Nancy jumped and looked like she might cry.

"There, there child," he said more softly, she was a young thing and Mrs O'Sullivan his housekeeper was training her well. "I do growl a bit," he continued, "but I won't cause a scene. In any case, Mrs O'Sullivan is bound to have the strength required to evict our trespasser. Run along now, do."

Nancy left the room and Mr Doyle helped himself to his breakfast. He ate alone, as he always did since his wife had died two years ago, accompanied only by the mezzo tick-tock of the large carriage clock which reigned over the mantlepiece. Briefly, he wondered who the woman on the drive might be. Last week it had been a buxom and bossy Mrs Walter Andrews and her sister Miss McArthur who had come from Reading on the train. They had each brought a meat pie and had eaten unabashed on the drive before ringing the doorbell and unashamedly asking Mrs O'Sullivan for a 'dish of tea' apiece.

The month before, Mrs Smith had brought assorted children who may or may not have belonged to her to gaze upon his house in St Albans. And the month before that a highly apologetic gentleman, a similar age to himself, had stood on his driveway alongside a wan young woman with wispy light ginger hair, whose pale grey eyes made limp full moons in her face.

"I can't believe this is the place, Papa," she whispered again and again to her father in the tones of a sleepwalker. When she had had her fill, her father took her by the waist and turned away from the house catching Mr Doyle's eye, from where he was watching the pair from a downstairs window. He nodded a nod of thanks to Mr Doyle, who found himself nodding back in approbation.

"Ridiculous," Mr Doyle grumbled out loud, with only himself and the clock to hear, and returned to his newspaper.

He had scarcely finished his coffee when Mrs O'Sullivan bustled in, her black silk skirt rustling and her lace collar slightly askew, the tiniest indication of ruffled sentiments.

"Excuse me, Mr Doyle," she announced as she entered, "but the lady on the driveway will not depart. I've done my best Mr Doyle, but I regret to inform you that either you will need to dispatch her yourself sir, or we will be forced to allow her to remain until she is ready to leave."

Mrs O' Sullivan was upset. She liked the house to run smoothly. Meals were always served at the same time every day and there was never a speck of dust to be seen on any surface. The linens were laundered to virginal perfection. Guests were received by invitation or at correct visiting hours. The stream of strangers who now appeared so regularly on the drive since Mr Dickens had published his dratted book irritated and annoyed her.

"Thank you, Mrs O'Sullivan, I'm sure you have done your best," Mr Doyle replied and stood up with a sigh. "We will probably have to leave the lady," he said. As he spoke he realised that the 'woman' who Nancy had referred to had become a 'lady' in Mrs O'Sullivan's opinion and thus his own.

This was surprising, Mr Doyle thought, so he decided that he would take a look at the person on his driveway for himself. From the drawing-room windows, he had a good view of the wide driveway and the gate and railings at the entrance beyond. The cherry tree in the centre of the drive was in full blossom, a heavenly dress of pink petals fluttering delicately in the simplest of breezes. He felt pleased that his attractive house was looking at its best today, despite the irritation of an uninvited visitor on the driveway beholding it.

He stood close to the dark red curtains of the study window and observed the lady. She was sitting on the gravel drive, her dark blue skirts arranged neatly around her. She wore a dark grey mantle and a dark grey bonnet fastened under her chin in a large bow with ribbons the same blue as her skirts. Her attire was neat and well-kept. Even a man such as Mr Doyle could notice that aspect of her presentation. The lady held a sketchbook on her lap. She was studying the house intently. Then she looked down and drew for a few minutes from her mind's eye, before renewing her gaze on the house. After a while, she stood up, smoothed out her skirts, and chose another place to sit, with a different angle of the house and a different view. She turned over the page in her sketchbook and commenced another drawing.

Mr Doyle was in a mind to leave her be and let her finish her sketch and depart, but something about the intensity in which she gazed at his house made him linger longer at his place by the window. Now that she had repositioned herself, he was less hidden from her view than he had been before. She saw him watching her and she smiled. He perceived that she was neither young nor old. Her smile was bright and firm. She smiled at him as if she knew him and had always known him. An involuntary tingle travelled from his neck to the base of his spine.

"Well there's nothing for it now," he thought to himself and went out onto his driveway to speak to the unknown artist.

"Good morning," he greeted her politely.

"Good morning," she replied and hastened to stand. "Thank you for permitting me to sketch your house, Mr...?"

"Mr Doyle. Mr Adrien Doyle," he replied looking at her pretty face made heart-shaped by the pull of the bonnet's ribbons and wondering at her age.

"I am, Miss Henry. Miss Millicent Henry."

"Pleased to meet you, Miss Henry," he said, thinking it was rather ridiculous to have such an introduction on his own driveway in front of his own house, but charmed nevertheless by her gentle manner.

She held out her sketchbook for him to see. He took the book from her hands and flicked respectfully through the pages. On each, was a black and white drawing of a building; here a house, there a workshop, here an inn, there a church, here a school, there a boat.

"I've been to almost everywhere he has written about and sketched the buildings," she said proudly.

The sketches were very good. Each was full of life and character. He had read some of Charles Dickens' work, not all, but at a glance he could match nearly every building to a story that he knew.

"These are very good!" he said passing the book back to her. Her crystal eyes were wide and hopeful as she took it, as if she was searching for praise that was not normally offered. He felt a lump come to his throat. He felt that what he would say next would be a great disappointment and that by saying the words something delicate and sensitive would be ruined, just as the petals of the cherry blossom would be ruined and crushed if caught underfoot once they had fallen to the ground.

"I'm sorry to tell you Miss Henry that this is not Bleak House."

Her eyes grew wide in astonishment and she looked around herself as if disorientated.

"But, Mr Doyle, what do you mean?" she cried. "There is a sign on the gateway that says this house is named Bleak House."

"Yes, my house is named Bleak House, but it is not the house that Mr Dickens described. He borrowed the name and the location, but the house in the novel he imagined from a property elsewhere."

She looked down at her sketchbook in sadness.

"I do feel rather silly now," she said in a small voice. "You must think me rather silly too."

"Not at all," he replied. In truth, when sitting at the breakfast table he had thought the unknown stranger rather silly. Standing by the curtain in the drawing-room he had thought her rather silly. But now he had met her on the driveway he did not have that opinion. No, here on the driveway he admired her.

"But it's a very good sketch Miss Henry, please do not be too disappointed."

"Thank you for your understanding, Mr Doyle. I had better leave now."

His heart lurched as she said this and he realised he did not want her to go. She ought not to go, not yet.

"There is no rush is there, Miss Henry? You have met my housekeeper, Mrs O'Sullivan, this morning, perhaps I could ask her to make some tea to refresh you and you could tell me about these other places you have visited."

At this Miss Henry's face brightened. It was unusual to meet someone so interested in her sketches as Mr Doyle appeared to be.

"Thank you, Mr Doyle," she agreed, "I should like to very much. I am due to return to my aunt's house on the Hatfield Road shortly, but I have time to take some tea with you."

Mrs O'Sullivan was decidedly put out when requested to provide tea for the lady who only a few minutes ago had been sketching uninvited on the driveway – and to serve it in the drawing-room at that. She decided to pour the tea herself rather than send Nancy in with the tray so that she could see with her own eyes what had caused the change in events. Her annoyance turned to surprise when she sensed the warmth of conversation between Mr Doyle and Miss Henry.

"What will you do with all these sketches?" Mr Doyle asked Miss Henry once the tea had been poured. "You know these are good enough to illustrate the books themselves."

Miss Henry's cheeks flushed a beautiful shade of rose at the compliment.

"Do you think so? Truly, do you think so?" she sought clarification that he meant what he had said and that his words were not empty praise.

"Yes, I do," he asserted.

"It is hard though for a lady such as myself to have illustrations published," she said sadly. "It is not something I waste my time thinking about. Instead, I have another plan."

"You do?"

"Yes. Do you see this?" she raised the ribbons of her bonnet to show him. He had not noticed before but they were embroidered all over with tiny pale blue forget-me-nots. "I embroider and I will stitch the sketches."

"Stitch the sketches?"

"Yes, I am creating a counterpane covered with a stitched sketch of each of the buildings that I have seen from Mr Dickens' books."

"What is the counterpane for," he asked, his brown eyes soft and voice full and rich.

"To share with my husband when I have one," she answered.

And for an instant, Mr Doyle saw himself under the Dickens' counterpane happily alongside Miss Millicent Henry, who had fortuitously visited the wrong Bleak House.

25.

GLADYS

Gladys had parked her elderly silver grey Honda in the far corner of the car park at Westminster Lodge. She reckoned it was the furthest space from the entrance, which meant that she would walk the most steps she possibly could from her car to the market and back to the car. More steps would mean a slimmer Gladys. When she thought about how tiny she had been as a little girl, how slim as a young woman and how round she was now that she had reached her middle years, she could hardly believe she was the same person.

"It's the change, Gladys," her sister Maybelline, who was even more generously proportioned around the middle than she was herself, had said to her in the Jamaican lilt which had never left her. "It can't be helped. And we're all big women in our family."

It was true, their mother, her aunts, and her grandmother too, before she had passed, were all large. All of them were lovely, friendly, warm women with comfortable bosoms to snuggle into and ample laps to be folded into when little. Their arms were open wide in embraces to cry into through the turbulence of adolescence and beyond, yet the same arms were firmly folded, rendering them immovable mountains, when their views differed from her own.

Maybe Maybelline was right. Maybe a thicker girth was the inheritance of hormone changes. She couldn't wait for the change to change. The flushes came when she least expected, leaving her hair soaked with sweat. She had lost count of the times she had woken in the night, her heart pounding with such ferocity that it felt like it was trying to escape from her body. Month by month her waist had become thicker and larger skirt sizes crept into her wardrobe.

But Maybelline's opinion was not that of her doctor's. Her GP had been sympathetic to Gladys' hormone plight. She had suggested HRT and Gladys took the leaflet home with her. The doctor was just as concerned with Glady's weight. "Pre-diabetes" she had said to her; "Reduce the sugar in your diet"; "Try to lose weight"; "You will feel better and sleep better too"; "Less strain on your joints". The doctor's list of benefits sounded like a shopping list. She knew that she'd find her work as a carer easier too. It could be such a physical job and she regretted that her excess weight had made moving around such hard work.

She suspected that Maybelline was wrong about the menopause making their waists larger. The family loved to come together and eat plates piled high with mouth-watering favourites dripping in fat. No one ever refused a desert when offered, that would be rude, and tea was always taken with sugar. Maureen, who Gladys went to every Thursday morning, was older than both Maybelline and Gladys and yet she was as thin as a reed. She couldn't be more than a size 10.

"That woman is thin because she is so sad and worried," Maybelline had said when Gladys mentioned it to her. "White women go thin when they worry." Again, Gladys wasn't convinced this was strictly true, but Maybelline was in no mood for contradiction. "I read it on the internet, Gladys!" she had declared, folding her arms up beneath her large breasts to signal no more was to be said on the subject.

Despite her sister's lack of support, Gladys had begun a new regime of walking and healthy eating. So far all was going well, she thought to herself, as she prepared to walk up Hollywell Hill to the market. Before her 'lose weight lifestyle' she would have parked her car in the closest car park to the market stalls. The new Gladys walked up the steep hill and carried all her purchases back down again. She didn't start work until 2 pm on Wednesdays, market day, so she had plenty of time.

Hollywell Hill is always steep, but to Gladys, it felt steeper than ever today. But the sun was out, a light breeze ruffled the leaves of the trees in the park alongside her and she was sure that her skirt felt a little less tight than last week. The abbey sat like a jewel in the crown at the top of the hill. As she walked up the hill she passed old cottages, interesting shops, attractive buildings of all ages. It struck her that when she had always parked in the car park at the top of the hill she had missed out on this pretty road. Sometimes it was nice to walk.

The market extended like a ribbon the length of St Peter's Street. Gladys chose a slight diversion around the clock tower because the route was pedestrianised and meant more steps. The first stalls she reached were the food stalls. The aroma of spices from the huge dishes of paella made her stomach rumble. Gladys pressed on determinedly. Next, as the street widened out and made room for the museum's outside café, came the bread stalls. She needed fresh bread and so she asked for two loaves. An assortment of French pastries stared tantalisingly at her from large stainless steel trays alongside the loaves of bread.

"Anything else?" the stallholder asked.

Gladys hesitated. She was feeling hungry. She looked at the trays wondering which had the least sugar. There was a flaky pastry that looked like a short bit of rope. That couldn't be too fattening, could it? Now, what it was called? It began with a 'c' or maybe it was a word with a 'p'. The unwelcome brain fog took all memories of any words for any pastries away from her. She pointed at the pastry she wanted.

"A croissant?" the stallholder questioned.

"Yes, please," Gladys smiled in relief that she had remembered that the pastry did indeed begin with a letter 'c'.

The stallholder picked out the croissant with a plastic-gloved hand and put it in a paper bag. Gladys took it. She would eat half of it when she had finished her shopping, before walking back down the hill to her car, and she would eat the second half tomorrow.

A little along from the bread stall was a row of greengrocer stalls. She had bought from them all before, so she didn't have a favourite. She passed each one slowly examining the products and the prices with her eyes, hovering a little behind the queue of those who had already decided what they wanted to buy so that she could take a good look but not be drawn in by a stallholder to say what she wanted before she was ready.

"Peaches £2 a punnet."

"Lovely strawberries, special offer."

"Broccoli 50p a head."

The stallholders punctuated the sales they were making with deep, loud cries, which gave you a jump if you were standing too close when they suddenly decided to advertise whatever produce their eyes rested on.

Gladys chose and paid for her salad, her vegetables and her fruit and filled her shopping bags until they bulged. The weight of the bags pulling through her arms added to her morning's work-out and the fresh produce she had bought would make delicious healthy dinners during the week, to offset the calories of the croissant. She looked regretfully down at the bunch of bright yellow bananas at the top of one of her bags, berating herself for buying the croissant and not thinking of having a fruit boost instead.

The market was busy. Shoppers buying their supplies for the week, or looking at stalls containing items which they liked but didn't necessarily need; handbags, clothes, picture frames, plants. Shoppers stepping from shop to market stall back to shop, and others hurrying past the stalls, giving them hardly a glance, intent on reaching an alternative destination – a bank, a pharmacy, a mobile phone store.

With her supplies for the week bought, Gladys decided that she would walk the full length of the market and see what all the traders had to offer. Her curiosity provided extra steps, burnt excess calories.

She paused at a clothes stall, a bright display of floating skirts, dresses, and blouses which fluttered in the breeze, the flowers in the fabric dancing like real wildflowers waltzing with the warm wind at the field's edge. She touched the fabric of a bright poppy skirt, feeling it with her fingers. It was a printed muslin, light and airy for a summer's day. A sign written in marker pen gave the price alongside the row of skirts; £15.

"I can do two for £28," a voice said mechanically from the shady recess inside the covers of the stall.

Gladys was tempted. The skirts were very pretty and a good price. She knew she was a size 18. No, she thought, not now, when I'm down to a size 16 it would be a treat.

"No thank you," she smiled at the young man and hurried on to the next stall on which an array of interesting wood carvings were on display: bowls, animals, boxes, door-stops.

The shopping bags were becoming heavier with every step that she took and her stomach was rumbling, urging her to eat her croissant, which having bought she really ought to consume, despite the healthy option of the bananas. She found a spare space of pavement in between the dress stall and the woodcarving stall, which no shoppers seemed to be using as a crossway. She put her bags at her feet and ate half the croissant, folding the paper bag over tightly when she had eaten half, and only half. The croissant made her feel better immediately. She hadn't realised how hungry she was and how much exercise she had done that morning. She picked up her bags and resumed her journey to the top of the market.

The fabric stall came next; a double stall with piles of fabric bolts stretched out. Gladys edged past slowly, admiring the quantity of fabric as much as the fabrics themselves. Fabrics for dresses, curtains, upholstery; fabrics for costumes, sheets, cushions. She wasn't a very good dress-maker, but Maybelline was. Gladys wondered if Maybelline could make a skirt for her more cheaply than she could buy one from the dress stall.

There was a new stall just past the fabric stall, one she hadn't seen before, nearly at the top of the market. It caught her eye while she was still thinking about fabrics. Hanging from a rail, which had been set up above a dark blue velvet cloth on the table, were shining, iridescent butterflies; colourful, bright butterflies; pastel, delicate butterflies – all attached to barely visible strings. The mass of butterflies bobbed up and down in the slight breeze, dancing joyously above the stall.

Gladys hurried over to look at them more closely and let her heavy shopping bags drop at her feet.

"They're lovely," she exclaimed reaching for one of the butterflies and feeling the lightest plastic, like streamers on a kite, beneath her fingertips.

"Hanging decorations, £8 each – two for £15," a man with a white beard behind the stall said to her.

Gladys thought of Howard and how much he would love the butterflies. Poor old Howard. He remembered less and less these days. She'd be going to his house tomorrow morning, she went every Thursday for 2 hours to give Maureen his wife time away from the burden of caring for him. It meant Maureen could have her hair cut, or do some shopping, see a friend. Howard adored butterflies. Now that he could leave the house less and less he had taken to drawing butterflies, covering sheets of paper in butterfly scribbles. When he had first started to draw his butterflies they were recognisable as flying insects with patterns and intricate colours. As the months had passed the patterns and the colours had disappeared, little by little, until now they were scarcely even flying triangles on his paper.

On the blue velvet tablecloth beneath the hanging butterflies, little boxes of butterfly jewellery were laid out. Earrings – butterfly studs and butterfly dangles; necklaces with butterfly pendants and butterfly beads; bracelets with tiny butterflies dancing from each link of the chain; bangles loose on the velvet, with coloured butterflies baked into the enamel or painted onto the wood. Such prettiness on the velvet dazzled Gladys. She picked up a necklace, took it out of the box, and watched the light reflect off the diamante wings.

"£12 each, two for £22.50," the man with the white beard commented.

"Thank you," Gladys muttered.

She picked up a bangle.

"£5 each," the woman sitting beside the white-bearded man said. She had sharp eyes and was looking at Gladys closely. This time there was no special offer announced with the price.

Gladys put the bangle down.

She had decided. She would buy a hanging butterfly decoration as a gift for Howard. She reached up to take one down; a stream of golds, oranges, and reds. Suddenly, she felt the familiar and hated woosh of heat surge through her body. It made her feel giddy and light-headed. She was heavy on her feet and lost her balance easily. She felt her heart beginning to race and sweat drip from her brow onto her face and around her neck. Instead of reaching for the decoration, Gladys found herself lurching for the table and as she did, she knocked half a dozen or so boxes of butterfly brooches and bangles to the floor. The boxes tumbled onto the pavement, the bangles rolled into the gutter. One even made its way, turning faster and faster, over and over, like an escaping wheel, towards the fabric stall where it was halted in its track by the shoe of a woman looking at fabric for a nightdress. The woman bent down, picked up the bangle, and returned it to the butterfly stall. A young man, holding a takeaway coffee, collected three bangles that had strayed into his path and put them back on the stall, with a nod to the white-bearded stallholder, before sauntering on his way.

Meanwhile, the white-bearded man's wife was busy picking up the scattered boxes from the gutter. She blew off the dust and checked that all the items were accounted for. She regarded Gladys with hostile eyes as if Gladys had caused the accident on purpose.

Gladys' face was now as much flushed with embarrassment as hormone change. She mumbled her apologies, wishing she was a hundred miles away from the market and the inadvertent fuss she had caused.

"Don't worry, my dear," the man said kindly reaching up for the butterfly decoration and taking it down for Gladys. He wrapped it in white tissue paper and took the money, while his wife placed all the boxes on the table, again making sure that the contents were all there, and eyeing Gladys suspiciously.

Gladys hurried back to her car. It was a long way – the entire length of the market, down the hill, and across the car park. Now she didn't care how many steps it took her. She just wanted to be back at home and change out of her sweat-soiled blouse.

Later that day, when she unpacked her shopping bags of vegetables and fruit she found, trapped between two bananas, a slim black bangle across which light pink butterflies danced. She removed it from the bunch of bananas. The bangle was so light almost to feel weightless. She slipped the bracelet over her wrist where it disappeared against her dark skin. The hostile eyes and tight lips of the butterfly stall holder's wife came into her mind's eye and annoyed her. Gladys took the remaining half of the croissant from its paper bag and ate it without thinking. Refusing to feel guilty about the croissant, she rummaged in her drawer for some pink tissue paper and, finding an old piece that was not too creased, she wrapped the bangle up and placed it alongside the white tissue covered decoration for Howard.

Thursday would bring two sets of smiles and it was a whole week until she would be back at the market.

EPILOGUE

MARCH 1349

I heard the little girl cry in the darkness. A small bundle in the corner of the stone cottage, she had covered herself in a thread-worn blanket so that she couldn't be seen, so that she couldn't see, and she pressed herself into the corner like a nut trying to retrieve the safety of the kernel. Even with her eyes tight shut, she could not obliterate the horrors of what she had witnessed and no amount of forcing her hands against her ears could deafen the sounds of what we had both heard. The blanket trembled with soft sobs.

Only two days before all had been well. I remember.

"Agnes, when you have done all that your mother has asked don't forget to milk the goat," her father had reminded her.

"Of course, father," she had replied with an angelic smile. All three of us knew that she would forget – she always did, and he'd already forgiven, her – he always did.

The child flew around the village assisting her mother with the daily tasks: a pot of honey for Uncle Matthew, borrowing a second-best shawl from Cousin Mary, nearly falling into the pond straining to see the emerging tadpoles from their jelly, returning the remainder of the yarn that her mother had borrowed to old-lady Isabel.

"How you do grow, child!" laughed her grandmother that morning as Agnes arrived with the spring sunshine and a loaf of fresh bread from her parents' oven. Kissing the wrinkled cheek, Agnes ran blithely back to her stone cottage to receive her next instructions, neglecting the goat, but not before quietly visiting the little blackbird family in the nest that I had shown her in the hedgerow.

Only two days ago.

The moaning had started that afternoon. By the evening, the cottage was filled with cries of pain. She had done everything she could for them. Brought water to drink, covered them with blankets. She did everything she could. I assure you, I watched her. She flew to her grandparents' cottage for help but the pestilence had reached there too. Uncle Matthew's door was closed and bolted. There was nothing the child could do. Fear held her by the throat and threatened to squeeze the life from her lungs. There was nothing she could do to stop the screaming and their pain, so she sobbed and huddled in her corner until there was dead silence and darkness.

"Agnes?" a small voice whispered, "Agnes, are you there?"

In the pale dawn stood a woman. Agnes could see her through the weave of the thin blanket. Cousin Mary. She lowered her blanket. Cousin Mary's watery blue eyes were streaming. She darted quickly into the cottage and pulled the little girl from the pit. The blanket tumbled to the floor and both fled to a home where there remained life for the present, leaving the front door to swing lightly in my April breeze.

MARCH 2020

I watched the little girl hold her mother's hand as she walked to school for the last time that morning. Although it was spring I was full of chill, so she wore her winter coat with knee-length socks, rather than knitted tights, as an acknowledgement that the daffodils had arrived. Normally, Anna would walk with a skip, plaits bouncing, chattering happily about school life, but today I noticed hesitancy, a shadow on her brightness.

"But Mummy, we will be able to go to Medieval Harmony, won't we?"

"I'm sorry, darling, I don't think so."

"But Mummy, you've paid the money and Miss Graham says that only people who don't pay can't go, and I remember you've paid."

Her mother smiled sadly – where to begin? How to explain?

"Yes, darling, Miss Graham is right about paying – under normal circumstances – but we've got to have a lockdown. We have to stay at home."

Tears welled up in her daughter's sad eyes.

"But Mummy, year 4 always go. I've been looking forward to it. We were going to sleep in stone cottages and learn how to bake medieval bread and weave cloth. We were going to dress up. Why can't we go?"

I examined the mother's face as she tried to reach past her worries into her thoughts. How should she tell an eight-year-old that she, her mother, the one who until now knew all the answers, now had no clue?

She squeezed her daughter's hand, knowing that this would be the first of many disappointments.

"I know how sad you must feel but we must keep safe and we must keep at home. Maybe you can pitch a tent in the garden and camp with your brothers?"

How delightful, I thought, what fun we will all have!

Anna nodded, and catching sight of her friend Maisie, ran quickly to the school door, waving her mother a hasty goodbye with a flash of her angelic smile.

Anna's mother turned away, sucking her bottom lip in to bite under her top as she did when worried. A replica school nature trip in the back garden was likely to be the least of her problems if the news reports were an accurate forecast – the creeping death toll, the line of coffins, all coming closer. A landscape and lifestyle changed when they reached the other side of this unknown.

She watched as I caught the cherry blossom in my breath and made it dance before her eyes, swirling and whirling like pink icing sugar snowflakes.

ACKNOWLEDGEMENTS

The stories in this book could not have been written without the patience and support of my loving family – Peter, Edgar, Rufus, Conrad, and Eloise. Thank you!

I am grateful to Peter Waine and Paul Harrison who both helped to take this book to a better place than it would have been without them; Fola Davies and Lucy Gravatt for their insights and wise comments; Carl French and Morgana Evans at The Endless Bookcase; Emma Harper, curator at the Welwyn-Hatfield Museum Service; and to Robert Voss, Lord Lieutenant of Hertfordshire.

Stephen Hill's map of 'Middle Hertfordshire' makes me smile whenever I look at it. It was a pleasure to work with him on the map to my book and a challenge to find the right century and even decade to illustrate. To avoid depicting the A1M, but to show the new town Welwyn Garden City, we chose circa 1925. Heartwood forest of course was not planted at this time, but we thought you would like to know where it would be.